DANGEROUS HARMONY:

Prelude

D. M. Cobray

Dion Blaine Publishing

Printed in the United States of America

First Printing: 2014

ISBN: 978-0615992297

Dion Blaine Publishing
1928 E. Highland Avenue – Suite F104-302
Phoenix, AZ 85016
dionblaine.wordpress.com

Cover Design by Prudence Lawrence
Interior Format by CL Foster

To Brandy M: For the inspiration.

1

Nichole and Crystal Titan

D.M. Cobray

"Nichole! Nichole! Listen to me! Girl, I am telling you! We need to get you back out there! You don't just stay down after a thing like that! You're too young! And way too *fuckin'* hot!"

The girl's voice on the phone was pleading and abundantly cheerful.

Nichole was so happy to have a younger friend like Kaylee. For the last year, she had gotten her through her darkest moments in her divorce from Scott: helping with the kids, doing her errands when she was sick, and just by being the best sort of twenty-something girlfriend a forty-year-old woman could ask for.

Now Kaylee was doing her best to lead her through the last few steps back into the land of the living. With the ink just dried on the divorce decree, it was time to go out and celebrate.

"I don't know, Kaylee. I think there'll be a lot of creeps there. I mean…I'd feel so out of place. I haven't been to a concert in…oh my God, twenty…"

"It doesn't matter! I see older people there all the time. People my dad's age! Even *older than you*!"

Well, that kind of stung. But really, it was reassuring that there actually were people even older than herself—and that some of them even went to concerts, presumably on walkers.

With the phone pressed up to her ear half-listening to Kaylee going on about how great Klankenshwetter and their singer Toby Barrett were, and how much fun their concert at the Ogden Theater in Denver would be, Nichole strode back to the bathroom mirror. There she was, in her gym shorts and an old T-shirt.

If she was *fuckin' hot*, she sure didn't feel it.

In fact, it just so happened that her T-shirt was from one of the last concerts she attended, back when she still felt *hot*. Maybe it was the absolute last time she felt hot. She looked at the shirt in the mirror, Kaylee's chattering still dancing on her eardrum.

Crystal Titans Hone the Cone Tour: 1991

That's what it said, emblazoned in red gothic script over a picture of a busty blonde Norse beauty holding a guitar, standing on the back of a Pegasus in front of a lightning storm.

My God, had it really been almost twenty-three years? Her mind went back to that concert and to that certain someone who still occasionally crossed her mind—even after all these years. The sounds, the smells, and the sensations she felt at Reunion Arena in Dallas before, during, and after—especially after. After, with him. All of that came back as she looked into the mirror.

Had it really been that long – almost a quarter of a century?

She looked into the mirror. Maybe she was a few pounds heavier. Gravity had started to show its effects on her in ways she had shrugged off. She still fended off passes at the grocery store and while shopping for furniture. She had her little barely-discernable pouch of skin at the bottom her belly—a souvenir of her two kids, whom she had fought long and hard to defend during the divorce. It was the divorce that had taken almost everything out of her and beat it on the pavement in front of God and everyone.

But straightening her back while jutting out her breasts and her still nicely-rounded bottom, she could still see a little bit of that girl just out of high school, feeling only joy for life and the world and willing to try anything. Well, almost anything, really.

Yeah, she still had a little of that in her.

"And we can go to LoDo's before and get some 151's, *baybee*! *Yeah*! Get kinda loaded and it will take the edge off. C'mon Nichole, you *need* this, girl!"

"Oh what the...*fuck*. OK, I'll go."

"Yay! I'll pick you tomorrow at seven after work! You're going to have a great time! And maybe you'll even get a young guy!"

"Oh, please…yeah, right …" That was just ridiculous.

"No! Nichole! They're all over women your age like a flies on shit these days. I mean like bees on honey…yeah. Oh…shit…I didn't mean …"

Nichole just laughed her ass off. That was classic Kaylee

*   *   *   *   *

The next evening found Nichole and Kaylee at a high-top table on the patio at LoDo's in downtown Denver.

The music was blaring in competition with the sports commentary from the dozens of TVs and the nattering of the masses of semi-employed hipsters and wannabes that surrounded them at the table.

Nichole felt totally out of place.

"Oh, this is going to be so great." Kaylee could tell that Nichole was uncomfortable, but at least she looked great. She was in her black leather miniskirt and a top that really showed off the goods. She had put makeup on for probably the first time in a year, and she had gotten her hair done in some sensual honey-brown ringlets. Kaylee sometimes seemed to take almost too much pleasure in hugging Nichole, but Kaylee told herself it was because she thought of her as the older sister she didn't have more than the mom she never really knew. Though sometimes she thought of her in other ways, as well: ways she didn't admit to Nichole.

"Yeah...*yeah!*" said Nichole over the music, snapping her fingers and swaying her shoulders, forcing some enthusiasm.

She looked out on the sea of people on LoDo's upstairs patio, all Kaylee's age or younger, standing around wearing things like checkered Vans, pants that were a few inches too short, and sunglasses they had found at truck stops or yard sales. Some of the girls were wearing outfits that looked like they belonged on Mary Tyler Moore in about 1972, but with the addition of Buddy Holly glasses. Most of them had distant, distracted demeanors, talking to each other while nodding in a variety of condescending know-it-all gestures. Others wore ripped t-shirts with unlikely logos on them from grain processing companies or whatever else made a minimum of sense given the context.

As she took a sip of the daiquiri that was strong enough to qualify as paint remover in some jurisdictions, Nichole felt her head start to swim.

Her mind went back to an all-ages club in a Dallas suburb in 1990. She had just turned eighteen and had been trying her best to get a fake ID through her cousin. But that suddenly didn't matter to her so much after she saw Crystal Titan that evening. The band was a local favorite that had already made some national waves with a guest shot on the Arsenio Hall show.

She remembered seeing him strut out on the

stage—the lead singer, Chad. She remembered being awestruck while giddily drinking a cherry Coke as he took the stage, all neon spandex and hair spray and eyeliner. Everyone back then was in neon spandex, and there was nothing but hairspray. The two together almost constituted a fire hazard.

Again, she looked out at the crowd at LoDo's: Beautiful young people trying their best to look neither beautiful nor young. So much had changed.

"Yeah...yeah...it's great!" she said half-heartedly.

After a slightly-buzzed visit to the ladies room, she and Kaylee were on their way out the front door. Kaylee stopped to talk to a co-worker she recognized, and while Nichole was waiting, a guy walked up to her. He was about in his early twenties, skinny, a little bit shorter than she, and wearing red jeans, a plain white T, and Miller High Life suspenders. On his head was a trucker hat advertising a plumbing company. He was holding a can of Pabst Blue Ribbon.

"Hey, I really like your shoes …" he said in a flat, slightly droning voice. Nichole smiled at his crooked glasses, semi-shaved head, and devil-like goatee.

"Why thank you!" she said, pondering oddness of this gesture.

"Are those the Jimmy Choo Vibes?" he asked.

"Uhh…*what?"*

"Your shoes: Are they Jimmy Choo Vibes? I think I know the model. They came out after the Evelyns. And there are still some who say those are the best ones. But …"

Nichole just looked at the guy and knitted her brows, then smiled at the notion that this might actually be some attempt at picking her up. "Actually, I got them at TJ Maxx."

At that Kaylee laughed, took Nichole by the hand, and waved off the funny guy in the hat. In short order they were down the stairs, out the door and into the backseat of a cab.

With her head swimming, the cab trundled along Market Street towards the Ogden Theater. Nichole looked out at the street life. It had been so long since she had been downtown on her own or otherwise.

Scott, her ex-husband, had been a homebody. He had been a good provider. Nichole had told herself she didn't care about going out. She didn't care about excitement. She had put away childish things. She had sworn off that sort of amusement and the other things she regarded as superficial in the interest of raising her two daughters. She wanted to show them how it was done: You grow up right, get a good enough education, and choose the right guy—the one who wants to provide: a serious man. And so she had stayed with Scott after choosing him while still in college. And in so doing, she had turned away from the guys she knew before—the body builders, the dancers, the tortured poets and songwriters, the druggies, and the rock singers.

One rock singer in particular.

It had worked as intended. Everything had been fine. She was happy, she had told herself, and she believed it right up until she happened to walk in on her husband's home office only to find him with his sweatpants around his ankles. He was sitting in front of his computer conducting a Skype session with one of their family friends—a woman who had gone to the protests against the common core curriculum with them, and had even stayed overnight in their guestroom when she said her husband had come home drunk and abusive. With one glance at the computer screen, Nichole got far more familiar with that woman than she had ever desired. One glance at Valerie Thompsen with a vibrator probing her vagina and her marriage to Scott was over.

Although Nichole had been faithful, over the years she had wondered about Chad from Crystal Titan, and whether he had been happy with the way his life had turned out. She would see him on Entertainment Tonight or Access Hollywood from time to time. He was usually with his statuesque Dutch wife, who had started out as a groupie and had gone on to do a spread in Penthouse, showing almost her entire digestive tract to anyone with $4.99 or a friendly older brother. She was happy for him. They had a couple kids themselves, she had heard.

During one segment of VH1's "Where are They Now?", she got a glimpse of their lifestyle. Chad had gone on to wisely invest his money from his two hits back in the 1990s: *How You Gonna* and *Shattered Hearts.* He had a chain of window-tint shops in Southern California. He was a multi-millionaire with a house in Bel Air. Every time she saw him, she'd remember what they were to each other back then. Or rather, what she thought she had been to him.

The cab let them off on Colfax in front of the Ogden. There was already a line out the door and around the block. There was a vibe in the air that took Nichole back decades. The kids looked different, but the ritual was the same. That same electricity hung in the air.

After a short wait they were inside and the show was about to start. Nichole giggled at getting carded for the first time in 20 years or more. She thought back on how she never did get her fake ID, and how it was still relevant in some way.

The Ogden was getting packed. Klank had quite a following, though the true faithful were those who still called them Klankenschwetter. Nichole heard a conversation between two fans nearby.

"Klankenschwetter's just not the same since they got signed, y'know?"

"Yeah, it's like they got real play on college radio, and they're getting to be like Hootie and the Blowfish."

"Well...dude, maybe not *that* bad."

After some announcements from the emcee about a collection for donations to the Sudanese refugees and a request to not spend the whole show watching it through the screen of a smartphone, and *especially* not an iPad, the lights dimmed, the crowd cheered, a guitar wailed, some drums hammered, and the show started.

Out from the side of the stage came a man still cloaked in boyishness. He was a redhead of about twenty or so, an acoustic guitar slung around his neck. A five-day growth showed on his face, and he wore a blue plaid shirt. Nichole looked at him and found him absolutely, radiantly beautiful in some way – in the way that had inspired some to call them "stars" in the first place. The crowd seemed to agree as they cheered him.

"Is that…?" asked Nichole as she patted Kaylee on the shoulder.

"*Yes! Toby Barrett!*" Kaylee was bouncing up and down.

The first song was a medium-paced number. It was a tribute to forgotten ideals called *Forget*. After the audience cheered, Toby took a little bow and addressed them.

"I know it's beautiful to be back here in Denver, and I'll tell you why: It's because I checked on my map once, and Denver is the *center of the universe*. Lots of love here! Thank you!"

And the crowd all cheered, even those who were still holding their phones up to their faces.

The second number was something about ecological disaster called *Scorched Earth*. It was darker and rocked a bit in a grungy way, but nothing compared to Crystal Titan.

Ahhh, Crystal Titan.

She remembered the thumping of dual bass drums, and lead guitarist JD Stonez shredding for five minutes straight while strutting across the stage, and the bass player well… playing bass. And then in front, always in front, was Chad. Reeling back, shaking his fist at the sky as he howled through *Satan Rain*. Acting like he was making out with JD during the title track to *Hone the Cone*, leaping off of amplifiers and doing splits in his green, yellow, or pink spandex tights, sometimes with ballet slippers, other times in low-rise cowboy boots or lace-up moccasins. She had a hand in picking out some of his outfits—if only for a while, back when they had been together and she was trying to make sense of what life on the road would be like for a nice girl like her.

But things were different back then.

These days, people couldn't even smoke at concerts. Instead of holding up lighters (which no one seemed to carry anymore) everyone held up their cellphones during the slow songs. And most of the kids seemed to wear things that would have gotten them laughed out of any concert back in 1990. Gone were the ultra-tight leather or spandex minis. Gone were the teased, sprayed hairdos and perms on boys and girls. Almost everyone looked like Arnold from *Little Rascals* now.

But then the third song started, and though it didn't rock, in its own way, it was a stunner. It started with Toby gently finger-picking a figure on his guitar. Then came the drums playing a varying rhythm pattern, and then Toby's voice softly massaged its way into the mix. At first it was like he was caterwauling, but as one listened, it became apparent he was interweaving this voice with the bass and his guitar in pure melody. And there was something in that song—the one called *Autoerotic Self-Immolation*—that enchanted her, possibly because it reminded Nichole of something from years before.

She started swaying to the slow but steady beat, and the notes traced the movement of her spirit. Suddenly it was 1991, back at the Reunion Arena. She was listening to the second encore the last time she saw Chad and Crystal Titan. There was a ballad they played called—strangely enough—*Nichole*. At most of the shows, they used it to close out their evening.

Kaylee looked at Nichole and nodded as she smiled, happy that she seemed to be finally getting into it.

And so the evening went. During *I Cheer for Nothing,* Kaylee insisted on taking Nichole by the hand and pushing towards the front row, through the standing crowd, until they were right up against the security barrier and center stage. They navigated through the sweaty, swaying bodies, with Kaylee pulling her along past the occasional sneer and eye-roll.

Then, during *Globalize your Discontent,* Toby set down his guitar and through the sad strains of a song about finding hope at the end of the world, it seemed he was singing directly to Nichole, gazing into her eyes while the words came:

> *Globalize, globalize, globalize*
> *Outsource your sadness*
> *Offshore your rage*
> *Find a cheap alternative*
> *Write on a different page.*

Nichole felt the temptation to turn away. It was almost too much just staring into his eyes. It seemed he had tapped into some reservoir of joy that knew no age. It felt eternal, though it likely only lasted a second or two. She felt him stare into some part of her that hadn't been seen in years. Her ex-husband seemed to so rarely look into her eyes after the first few years of marriage. That was OK. For almost twenty years she had told herself that it was OK; he was a good provider. It was OK that she and Scott didn't share that connection she had felt with Chad before. It was all OK.

But now she was feeling what she had felt with Chad again, but with this young man in his plaid shirt and ripped jeans and stubbly face, standing five feet in front of her while singing in his own quirky way about acknowledging and accepting disappointments in life, and making the best of what remained. She looked into his eyes and felt something familiar, something that reminded her of the pure elation she had felt at one time. In Toby's eyes she found hope that the best was yet to come, regardless of the drab nature of his lyrics.

After eight more numbers, the show had reached a fever pitch, but Nichole was feeling the strain of standing on the concrete floor in her TJ Maxx heels for over two hours. The elevation of being at the concert – the feelings of hope and reclaimed youth and elation – were almost not enough to offset the agony of high heels. She wandered a bit through the crowd, feeling the occasional stranger's hand against her ass or brushing against her tits. It wasn't as scary as she thought it would be — just part of the experience.

When she looked around she found she had drifted a few rows away from Kaylee. She noticed a large, smiling black man in a shirt marked "Security" talking to Kaylee over the sound of one of the encores.

Kaylee looked over at Nichole and pointed, an expression of delight coming over her face as she bounced.

Ah, this was something Nichole remembered from the old days: Kaylee was being called backstage. Well, that made sense. Kaylee was twenty-six and stacked and cute, with her little aerobicized hips and thighs and her tits propped up inside her little short cocktail dress. It was understandable. She could have some fun backstage with the band, and Nichole could just get a cab ride back home.

Well, this was fun, this concert thing, she thought to herself.

"Ma'am, Toby and the band would like to invite you backstage for a little party if you'd like to go," said the security guard, almost shouting over the amplification as the band pumped out *I am Only a Social Construct.* "My name's Tyler. Your friend says you're Nichole, right?"

"Yes, thank you, but she can go. Don't need to

22

bring me along. I'll be fine. That's OK."

"No ma'am, I don't think you understand. Mr. Barrett requested you. Just you. Your friend can come along, too, but he told me to ask you. Lady in a black skirt and the red blouse with the design on it. He didn't mention her."

Nichole looked at him. He had a gentle and sincere expression. She couldn't believe it. She looked over at Kaylee, whose eyes were almost popping out of her head with glee as she bounced in happiness for her friend.

Tyler offered his hand to Nichole and opened the gate. Kaylee wedged past a few hipsters, and suddenly they were both walking towards the backstage area along the security corridor, both jeered and cheered at by the audience in the front row.

*   *   *   *   *

Kaylee waxed ecstatic about their good luck and the excitement that awaited them from outside of the bathroom stall door. Nichole told herself she was ready for whatever awaited her in the VIP lounge.

The VIP courtesy suite was about the same as what Nichole remembered from her days with Chad back in those Crystal Titan days. There had been a lot more cigarette smoking back then, and apparently, a lot more hard drugs. Back in the day there would be a bunch of party food waiting for the band: Doritos, Cokes, and hotdogs. Now there was a table of organic hummus and veggies with bottled water.

Nichole sat on the filthy couch next to a dreamy young woman who introduced herself as Chazz. She stared at the TV playing reruns of *Seinfeld*. Chazz didn't bother looking Nichole over. She was wearing an apron dress, had dreadlocks, and smelled like strong pot.

"Are you with the band?" asked Nichole cheerfully.

"Ummm...yeah...I'm Grant's girlfriend, I

guess…y'know…the bassist."

"Not Toby?" asked Nichole.

Chazz squinted, then softly laughed in a muted way. "Oh no, that guy…he's so fucking uptight you could make diamonds in his ass." She left it at that and went back to watching TV.

A few minutes later, there was a commotion as the door opened and the band entered. First the drummer, then the bassist, then the guitarist, and then Toby Barrett.

Nichole's eyes met his again. He smiled in this adorable man-child way as his eyes met hers. He was talking with some roadies about the show as the room suddenly got very noisy.

"Hey, how are you? Did you like the show?" She remembered the guitarist from the band. He introduced himself as Cal. He looked cute, with dark, deliberately messy hair and five-day beard growth. He had gauge piercings in both ears that made it look like he had bottle caps or Necco wafers in his earlobes.

"Yeah you guys are great! What a show! I haven't been to one in ages!"

"Oh yeah? Thanks! Well you look great. I'm surprised you don't get around more."

"Well thank you!" Nichole blushed at the attention.

"You should consider travelling with us," he said, offering her a bottle of expensive spring water.

"Oh no! I've got kids. I couldn't do that."

"Oh, like, little kids?"

"Not that little. Two daughters. Thirteen and sixteen."

Cal looked a little confused. "Well, if you don't mind me asking...if this isn't rude... how old are you?"

"I'll be forty-two in June," said Nichole, trying not to let her blush show as a smile overtook her lips.

At that, Cal dropped his bottle of water.

"Oh wow...just wow...I thought...wow."

"How old are you?" she asked.

"Well, I'll be twenty...soon."

And all Nichole could do was to laugh at the whole situation.

But they sat down together and had a good conversation about music and how the industry had changed. Cal took Internet-based college classes in environmental engineering on the road. At some point or another, he leaned over and put his arm around her back. It was comfortable and sweet. As the conversation continued, he placed a hand on her knee, which was friendly. And at some point, she felt Cal's cheek against hers, his bottle-cap dangling near her face, and his hand working its way up her bare thigh.

And then she started to remember those days back with Crystal Titan, and how she constantly fought others impression of her being one of *those* girls. A groupie. Pussy for the band. She was only interested in Chad at the time, but the more time she spent around the band, the more certain things were expected of her.

As Cal gently nuzzled her cheek there on the filthy couch, Nichole looked across the room at Kaylee, who was dancing with the drummer, grinding her hips and ass up against him as his hands snaked up and down her torso. He lifted a joint to her mouth and she took a hit. She looked at Nichole and smiled. She turned to shotgun it back to her newfound lover, whose hands gently rose to cover her breasts.

Nichole looked down to realize that her nineteen-year-old acquaintance was taking a few liberties himself, nuzzling her neck and feeling her right breast.

Was it too late? Chad had chosen the Dutch groupie over anything Nichole could offer. She thought back and considered that she had been so tight, so controlled, and so stingy with her affections. And look what it had gotten her: twenty years of housework and sparse sex with a masturbating sales manager in a boring little two-story in Arvada.

She looked at Kaylee again, showing nothing but youth and pleasure and confidence, jutting her ass up against the drummer's pelvis as he flexed against her. His hands ran through her hair as rap music played in the background and the smell of pot got stronger.

Nichole felt Cal gently move her chin to face him. At once his lips were upon hers, and his hand worked to squeeze her warm, full breast. She felt his tongue touch the edge of her lips, and she allowed her mouth to be opened, gently.

"Hey, Cal, bro ..." she heard a voice that had become familiar, only very recently. "Maybe you should...you know...there are those two over there. They're really nice." Cal gestured to two girls who looked to be in their early twenties, standing near the snack table with red Solo cups in their hands. Cal was disappointed and he was trying to be angry. It was so against the principles of Klankenschwetter to be so possessive, or whatever was being laid on him at this point. Toby could be such a fucker.

Toby looked at Nichole and smiled, then flexed his neck, smiled, and winked at Cal in a way that said "give me a break on this one and I'll make it good later."

Cal looked back at Nichole while slowly unwrapping his arms from her. "Well, looks like I have other things to take care of. Nice to …" and he leaned forward and kissed her tenderly again, in a kiss that seemed to go on just a little too long. Maybe Toby tapped him on the shoulder. But he got up eventually, and Nichole instantly felt something missing. Her head was swimming. She glanced over at Kaylee, who was now giggling and fully embracing the drummer as he squeezed her tits.

Then Toby was next to Nichole.

"So," she asked wryly, "is Cal your opening act? Your warm-up man?"

"Sometimes," he smiled. "Sometimes I'm his. It's an equal arrangement. We're all about equality," he said, with something between humor and smugness.

"I noticed from your lyrics," said Nichole. "Too bad you forgot the joy."

Toby knitted his brows and shook his head disbelievingly. "What do you mean? I think we're all about joy. The joy of music."

Nichole laughed. "Toby, the joy of music is about joyous things, not globalization or chemical leaks. I don't really know what you're going for there, but it's not joy."

Toby was caught a little off-guard, but he felt something new about Nichole as he looked her over. She was much more than a luscious older woman of the sort he had determined earlier in the year would be his next conquest.

"We're about finding hope through adversity. You know, being realistic. I mean, what do you consider to be joyous music?"

"Music from my generation. We could listen and just not make a big deal about it. Music was for a good time, pleasure, you know. Not to make some political point or to show someone up for being …"

"Your generation? What do you mean? You mean our generation? Yours and mine?"

"Don't give me that, please. I mean thank you, but you know I'm older." Nichole squinted and shook her head, but she was no less charmed.

"Not that much older. I mean, I'll bet you liked Hootie and the …"

Her face suddenly boiled with rage. "Fuck you!" she said simply. She got up to leave.

"Nichole, please…no c'mon, I was just …" said Toby. Nichole was already halfway to the door. "Look, look…I am sorry." he said. All eyes in the room were on them, and Cal and Grant were making mooing noises in a teasing way.

Nichole stopped in her tracks. Toby walked up to her from behind, slowly.

"How old are you, Toby?" she asked.

"I'm twenty one," he said.

Cal piped up. "*Too young! You're a fucking amateur! No game!*" Toby waved at him dismissively and sneered at him with the corner of his mouth.

"Twenty one, eh?" Nichole crossed her arms and turned around. "Well, around the time you were born, I was part of the scene. I knew the guys who were the center of it. And the music was all about feeling the world's joy and rocking out with passion, and not just suffering with its pain. That's where I'm from. It's not *Hootie* and the *Fucking Blowfish!*"

Toby gently took her hands and drew her towards him. His blue eyes gazed into hers. He smiled.

"I know you're older. I was just fucking with you."

"Well don't! Not if …"

"Not if what?" he asked softly. Nichole felt her hips moving involuntarily. Her breasts felt tight in some way that was vaguely familiar.

"Not if …"

"Not if what?" He moved closer to her. His hand dropped to her hip.

"Not if …"

And his lips were upon hers.

She heard cheering and jeers in the background. She looked over at Kaylee, whose dress was now lowered, revealing her pert and tanned young breasts to the room.

Nichole felt her body falling against Toby's

now. They embraced each other, and they staggered together towards a door leading off to a sideroom. As Nichole walked into the room, Kaylee waved, smiled, and whooped.

In the room were two single beds and a small table and lamp. Toby was showing a vastly greater amount of experience than his twenty-one years would suggest. He guided her to the bed, his hands working all of the best spots. Nichole felt a tingling in her pelvis that hadn't really been there in so long. Soon, her top was over her head, and she felt a surge of excitement as her bra fell away, revealing her luxuriously large breasts and fully erect nipples. Toby's mouth fell to one then the other as his right hand slipped up her thigh, slowly approaching her sex. He moaned with desire.

Toby's arms were strong around her, guiding her to where he needed her to be for not only his pleasure, but her pleasure, as well. It seemed that he had all the right combinations. As his tongue gently darted into her mouth, she felt his hand caress her wet sex through her soaked panties. He was somehow pleasuring her mouth, her breasts, and now her pussy all at the same time. She fell back on the bed. He pulled off his T-shirt, revealing a young and muscled bare chest. He reached forward and up her skirt. She lifted her ass enough for him to get her panties off.

Oh, what's happening? Could this really be ...

Nichole was amazed at the turn of events. Here she was, the mother of two teenaged girls in the National Honors Society, a good suburban housewife-turned-divorcee. And on her first night out in years, she was on the verge of fucking a rock star. A very young rock star.

But he didn't get right down to business, exactly. He was proving to be a true gentleman.

Her panties slipped down her thighs, and Toby showed that he was as talented with his tongue as he was with his voice. He started with a soft, flat tongue on her, just beneath her clit. He lapped at her lips, sucking in her juice and growling softly with pleasure. Nichole heard her own voice, raspy and breathy, moaning with him as he drank from her fountain of life. It seemed to last hours. It could have lasted hours, and she would have loved every second.

Then she felt him work his fingers into her velvety cavern, flexing, flip-flopping gently and passionately inside of her while he sucked gently on her clit. In a moment, a white-hot surge of pleasure filled her entire body, undulating and flipping up and down her spine and seemingly out the top of her skull. It was heavenly. He lay next to her while the roller coaster of her own orgasm lifted her. He lay next to her and beheld her in her everlasting moment of pleasure.

Nichole looked at him and smiled. He smiled back. Her hand went down to his pants. She tried to unzip him, but it got awkward and she laughed. He laughed as he undid his belt and lowered his pants. He wasn't the largest she could remember, but he was pretty close to the nicest, and though she hadn't done it in longer than she could remember, there was something drawing her towards his thickness.

With him on his knees on the bed, she leaned forward and took him in her mouth. Licking the sweet pre-cum from the fat purple head, his cock jutted upwards at something like a 45-degree angle, which was something she hadn't seen in years. She hungrily took him in her mouth, feeling his length surge against her tongue as it flexed with every heartbeat. His hands gently wove through her hair. Out of the corner of her eye, she noticed something.

There in the mirror was Nichole Drake, formerly Jenkins—forty-one years old and a mother of two teenaged girls, a member in good standing of the HOA board for her subdivision, an account manager for a cell phone company with one great client in HammerCo Investments (where they loved her), faithful church attendee, and she was literally sucking the youth out of a boy young enough to be her son, whom she only knew as the front man for a band she hadn't heard before that evening.

And she would have: She wanted his seed in her, somehow.

But Toby had different ideas. He turned her around and laid her on her back on the bed, taking a moment to slip a condom on his thick, pulsing cock.

Nichole was powerless. She wanted it all. He licked and sucked her nipples as he moved between her legs. His cock sank into her wet, hot folds. He gasped as he entered her, and she felt his full length press all the way up to her cervix, where no man had been since she sent her husband packing a year before. And as he let the thick, throbbing head of his cock steep within her wet, grasping pussy, she felt something new rising up within her—or rather, it was something old and very familiar that he had brought back to her. There was something in the way he moved and the motions he used that she recalled from years before. It was as though everything about his physicality bespoke a certain rhythm and awareness of harmony. He brought her legs up on his shoulders and pounded deep within her, the headboard bouncing off the walls behind her. He panted and groaned. He held her arms down. She felt exposed and conquered as he ravaged her with his hard cock, his full balls slapping against her ass, his thighs straining hard against her as he tried his best to fully enter her with every stroke. Sweat dripped from his brow, and she felt a tension building within her for the second time that evening.

He got back up on his knees and motioned for

her to follow. She rolled over, but had almost forgotten what to do. Scott had only prodded at her half-heartedly from behind once or twice through their twenty years together. But Toby showed his experience by having Nichole press her legs together and arch her back, pressing her rear out towards him. He entered her from behind, then gathered her hands together, pinning her arms behind her back. He moved his thighs on either side of her and slowly built momentum, rapidly hammering his cock up into her wet, throbbing vagina as he began to howl.

After grunting and wailing for what seemed like an eternity of pleasure, she heard him gasping with each breath. *"Now... now... Nichole... my...beautiful..."* and she felt her own waves of white-hot pleasure surge within her. She felt him ramming impossibly fast and hard as his cock flexed up in her. They gasped and moaned as one.

And Nichole collapsed in a hot, spent mess, and Toby gently fell on her, their sweat intermingling.

*   *   *   *   *

Very early the next morning, a black executive sedan pulled up outside an unassuming two-story house in Arvada. A door opened. Nichole carefully pulled herself upright as she exited the backseat. She tried to tip the driver, but he told her he had been taken care of.

The sun was just coming up. Kaylee still sat in back. Nichole had been texting with Toby for the entire ride from the Warwick hotel downtown, alternately thanking him, teasing him, and rejecting-though-not-rejecting his offers to take her to Dallas with the band for their next show in a few weeks. She had been reading the texts to Kaylee, and they had both been giggling like schoolgirls.

Kaylee had leaned against Nichole and nuzzled against her breasts in a way that seemed friendly and silly. Or maybe a little more than that. Kaylee tenderly kissed her as she got out of the car and told her to call. Nichole thanked her for the experience of her life. She sprang up the stairs with a light step, her TJ Maxx shoes in her hand.

Nichole still had a smile on her face as she quietly opened the front door. She snuck into the bathroom to look at herself again, trying to avoid making any noise that would wake her two daughters.

In the mirror, there was a woman wearing a concert T-shirt -- a new concert T-shirt. This one was styled with a giant kale leaf behind all the concert dates for Klank. Or Klankeschwetter, rather. Maybe. Though the shirt did say "Klank." She had forgotten to ask Toby. She wasn't sure what to call them, or what she was entitled to call them, rather.

And then she looked more closely in the mirror, appreciating her smudged makeup, her just-been-fucked hair, and the slight flavor of Toby's second orgasm still on her tongue. And she laughed.

She had been a silly, gloriously absurd bitch. And she was full of life and joy. And a little bit of Toby.

After a long shower, she managed to get a few

hours sleep. When she awoke she put on a bathrobe and went downstairs to face her two daughters. There was nothing like doing the walk of shame in front of one's own flesh and blood.

"So how was it, Mom?" asked Madison, the sixteen-year-old.

"Oh it was great, honey. Yeah. Yeah ..." she said, noticing her ears were still ringing as she smiled. She poured a cup of coffee and stirred in some Splenda.

"Did you meet any guys?" At thirteen, Chloe was inquisitive and boy-crazy.

"Oh not really. No, hon. Those guys are so...they are so...you know...not right. They are like so creepy and flaky...so I ..." Nichole needed to dissemble for the sanctity of her two daughters.

"Yeah I know what you mean," said Madison. "At least you got to hear Klank. And they are sooooo good, Mom. I mean, I am soooo happy you got to hear them. I wish I could have gone with you."

"Well maybe next year. Kaylee and I just …"

"I mean, Mom, I like them so much I'm doing a research project on them for school. I'm learning everything about them because they are soooo relevant."

Nichole started thinking how she could help her daughter get inside information from sources that she probably couldn't quote on a report for her Junior-year project at Arvada High. She smiled and took a sip of coffee.

"I mean," she continued, "it's even about generations and stuff. I mean, intergenerational. I mean, that's relevant to today, you know?"

"Well, yeah, I guess I wasn't the only old person there. Certainly not the oldest."

"No, but I mean something different, Mom. It's like…this is sooo deep…I mean…let me read it to you." Madison picked up her iPad and started reading something from a Wikipedia article

"Members of Klank can trace their roots to parents with previous success in the music industry. Drummer Dave D'Angelo's father played bass with Arraignment, a fixture on the LA punk scene in the 80's, while lead singer Toby Barrett's father Chad Morris scored with two hits as a founding frontman of hair-metal rockers Crystal Titan... ."

Nichole's coffee cup crashed to the floor and shattered.

D.M. Cobray

2

The Angels Harp

D.M. Cobray

The summer sun had just retreated beyond the mountains to the West of Las Vegas. The last of the beautiful colors from the smoggy sunset still lingered. It was family hour.

A text message popped up on her iPhone. Her heart fluttered

"Can you meet now?"

"Now? Where are you?"

"In your backyard by the trees."

Oh. My. God.

Allie looked at the last message on her phone.

Six words. Just a text. But that's how this had all started. Just a text. Now look at her. A trilling feeling ran across the soles of her feet and concentrated around her toes.

"Give me a few mins."

She looked up from the phone. Annabelle and Brendan were on the floor in front of the TV. SpongeBob was agitated about something. That was rare. He was usually so mellow, happy-go-lucky. It had something to do with Sandy Squirrel. Sandy was in her bikini.

She wondered what it would be like for a squirrel and a sea sponge to…you know. Oh, that was ridiculous. Why was she thinking that way? On second thought, she really didn't need to wonder why she was thinking that way.

"OK, kids, time for bed."

They looked at her. It was barely eight o'clock. "But *Mom*!" They said in unison. They had been practicing.

"No, off to bed. You have a big day tomorrow. You have soccer, and Annabelle has …" She had to think. "Annabelle has an important thing we're going to do that will be very fun."

Brendan furrowed his nine-year-old brow and flexed his red crew cut. "Swimming?" he asked.

"Yes! Swimming. Swimming. You need plenty of sleep for that, little girl! I'm going to wake you up early."

They groaned. "Can't we watch the end of the show? Please?"

Well, that was a nicer response than just "*No!*" combined with a tantrum. She could work with that. Maybe she was negotiable tonight. It was amazing how negotiable and flexible she had proven to be—despite her better judgment—gain and again. She pursed her lips.

"How much time is left?"

Brendan hit the button on the DVR remote that displayed remaining time. "Only six minutes," he said.

"OK, watch the end of this, and then off to bed."

Allie got to her feet.

Why did it have to be tonight? Why this night, when she was wearing sweatpants and her late husband's college football jersey? She couldn't remember if she had shaved, which meant that she probably hadn't. She was still in the habit from her years of marriage to Barry, but that habit was slipping away. He had demanded that she always be naked there. The new guy didn't seem to care that much.

As she walked past the kids, she wondered what they knew. What could kids sense about a thing like this? Nothing. Mom was just in a mood. That's all. She felt her steps tighten as she strode across the carpet and towards the master bedroom.

She flicked on the bathroom lights.

Oh dammit. Ugh. Well...it would be dark out there.

She looked at her hair. It was like a mop. It was a mommy cut—short enough for easy care.

Whenever she dropped the kids off at St. Viator, she could look through the windows of every BMW and Volvo and Lexus SUV and see the same haircut, some of them accented with a hairband. *Nice try, sister, with your little girlish flourish. You're pure suburbia, just like m*e. Looking back on missed opportunities and taking whatever pleasure uncertain life here in Masterplanville, USA offers: bake sales, barbeques, cheap new tchotchkes in the housewares department at Target, the annual community rummage sale, maybe a family vacation to some "-land" or "-world" or another. *You're all about the kids now, sister. Anyone can see it with a single glance at your hair.*

Allie pulled her hair back and looked in the mirror. At least she wasn't going grey. It was sad enough being a widow at her age. It would have been devastating to be a grey-haired as well.

Poor Barry. She was just so glad that if it needed to happen, that it was while he was on duty as a compliance officer for HammerCo. The extra insurance payout for his on-duty death during a business trip had ensured that she didn't have to worry about finances – at least not for a while.

Would the kids notice if she did a little ponytail? Probably not. Not the sort of thing they noticed. But they would definitely notice a change in clothes, and given Brendan's occasional restlessness it was way too risky to change into anything more appealing and practical for the purpose. No tennis skirt. No flowing gauzy caftan with the open neckline—the one that almost looked like loungewear lingerie. Mommy was already in her pajamas. If anything was going to happen in the backyard, it would be in sweatpants and a jersey, and he'd just have to accept it.

It almost galled her that she was certain he would.

Lipstick, maybe? No. A little eyeliner? No. Tinted Chap Stick? No. No. No. She could hear

Annabelle already: "Mommy, why you wear make-up now? Can I wear some?"

No. No. No. No.

She looked in the mirror. She still felt his caress on her cheek. She still could see the way he'd gazed at her. He'd tell her stories—stories about St. Claire and St. Theresa and St. Lucy. He'd compare her to the beauties of paintings and statues in Rome—depictions of the saints. And then he'd tell her she had eyes that Katy Perry wished she had. That always made her laugh. From the sacred to the profane—that was his charm. He liked Katy Perry. He liked the compact, busty brunettes. He liked her.

She smiled in the mirror, but she was trying to look at herself through his eyes. She looked and saw something of what he saw, as much as she could. Something kept him coming back. Something made him keep risking, well...everything.

She heard the SpongeBob theme ending. The show was over.

"Off to bed!" she yelled. She shut the door. There was one important thing to take care of first. Might as well do it now. Only took a minute.

"OK kids, off to bed! Come, come, come!"

And she helped Annabelle into her nightie and tucked her in, hearing tales about something Katrina did in school that upset her and how she wanted to have a Dora the Explorer bouncy-house for her birthday party. She kissed her on her forehead, and then turned out the light. On the way back to the living room, she stopped off at Brendan's room and did the same, though she had noticed him submitting to her motherly care less and less all the time. He was looking more like his father every day.

Soon his father would have needed to have a talk with him. Tell him about life. He *would have* needed to. As soon as Brendan's door crept shut and latched, she felt her back straighten and her legs stiffen. Her steps were measured but quick.

"You are a precious moon flower to me," said

the text waiting on the phone. Allie smiled.

"Your precious flower will need a few minutes still. Kids just in bed now."

"I'll wait :-)" came the immediate reply.

Allie flicked through the program guide. She selected an episode of *Seinfeld*. She remembered when it was funny, back when she saw it the first time, all those years ago. It was still kinda funny.

Time, time, time.

On came an ad for a profile on VH1 of a new band called Klank and how they used to be called Klankenshwetter. What a name! They looked good, though. It sounded familiar, maybe kinda like Hootie and the Blowfish. Maybe she'd get their album at Target if they had it when she was there next.

She waited to hear noise echoing in the hallway. Brendan was still softly knocking his knee against the wall. Or maybe he was masturbating. No…he was too young for that, she thought.

By the first commercial break, the noise had stopped. She risked walking back to make sure Annabelle hadn't gotten out of bed again to play when she should have been sleeping. Allie gazed into her room from the hallway. Just her little angel curled up in bed. Her blanket fell and rose with her breath. Brendan's door was still closed.

OK. Now. Go.

Allie made her way through the kitchen and past the cat that glanced at her from the counter. The cat knew. Cats always know but never tell—provided you give them a little incentive. Allie would forget she saw the cat on the grey granite countertop, munching the philodendron, in exchange for her silence.

Out into the backyard, past the pool and the lawn furniture, over the grassy expanse she had mowed for Barry on weekends when he'd be working out of town. She still mowed while thinking of him a year after the accident that took his life. She exhaled.

And there, under the tall, broad ficus tree, just barely visible as a silhouette—there he was.

He had been watching her from the time he heard the patio door slide open. He took a step forward and wrapped his strong arms around her. Her lips rose to his. She felt his hands stroking her back and sides, from her shoulders down to her ass. As his hand curled to squeeze her behind, his head slowly and sensuously turned, and his tongue darted to meet hers. He pulled her closer. She arched her back slightly to press her breasts against him, to feel his muscular chest. A hand rose from her ass up her side and petted the side of her breast, the thumb searching for her nipple. Found. They were hard to miss, especially in her current state. His hips flexed and she felt him. The poor thing! How long had he been out here this way?

She reached down towards his belt with one hand, her lips still pressed against his. He wanted her enough to risk coming here, only to stand waiting outside, where someone might have seen him. And she couldn't believe she was thinking this way, but she thought one gift deserved another. Her hand pulled at the belt, then she felt his gentle, smooth, soft hand touching hers, stopping her. Their lips parted.

"Allie, I came here for you." he said, gazing into her eyes.

Gently, he turned her and backed her up toward the tree trunk. It was like they were dancing again. She remembered feeling the energy from him that time, that silly little twirl he gave her at Brendan's 4th grade sock-hop. It was a surprise, more of a joke than anything. It lasted seconds and ended in laughter. That was months ago.

She suddenly felt she was nothing, nothing like those other shorthaired moms dropping off their kids at St. Viator. Short hair or no.

There was a romantic little bench in white wrought iron setting beneath the tree, one where Allie would sit and read sometimes. She felt the backs of her knees contact the bench. She knelt down and took her seat, and he knelt down before her. He kissed her again, leaning forward and tilting his head to more intimately penetrate her with his tongue. Their tongues expertly played each other. His hands roamed from her hips up her sides and felt her full breasts through the jersey. His thumbs and forefingers again found her nipples standing at attention, begging for contact. His hands sank and found their way under the jersey, creeping up past the soft, barely-protuberant mommy belly that he seemed to love but which still was a source of embarrassment to her: something to be attacked sometime with Pilates and a strict diet. His warm hands caressed her as they rose up her torso. They gently grasped her breasts. This man, those soft hands. She shuddered. The jersey rose above her breasts, and panting he broke off the kiss.

Oh, why did it have to be tonight? I haven't even shaved ...

His head lowered to her left breast. He held her hips tightly. His other hand squeezed a handful of her, and suddenly his lips were on her, his tongue circling and teasing the thick, pink nipple. He sucked sweetly. With his other hand, he was lightly drawing lines around her areola, tracing his nails and fingertips, occasionally lightly pinching and squeezing. She felt her legs getting rubbery. She knew she was even wetter than she had been in the time since he texted half an hour before.

Where did he learn this? How does he…

She was doing it again. She reminded herself to forget who he was, just go with it.

His hands slowly released her breasts. They traced down her sides and came to rest at the elastic of the sweatpants. His fingers crept underneath. She placed her hands on his. *Oh no! Here? Now? But I …*

He looked up at her. "Allie, I came here for you."

"But…but……" Her throat was dry. He looked into her eyes and placed his index finger to his lips. Then his hands gently moved hers away from the elastic. She lifted up as he slowly slipped the sweatpants down over her thighs, the ones he made feel so beautiful, and took her cotton panties down with them.

But I haven't shaved…

He closed his eyes and slowly leaned forward, his right hand caressing and exploring her mound. Her knees shook. She felt his fingers on her lips. He traced her slit. And the sensation was amazing as she felt his breath on her inner thighs as he leaned forward, and his lips finally contacted hers.

Allie shivered and gasped. She heard herself moaning, her own breath shuddering. He parted her lips with his tongue, using his fingers to expose her slightly. Then his left hand went down to her calf, and without moving away, he tapped to signal her to step out of her pants. She complied, and then thought about what she had just done and where she was. What would the kids or the neighbors or a police helicopter see if they were suddenly discovered? Mrs. Allison Donahue in her backyard, minus pants but still wearing gym socks, and a handsome man—this handsome man in particular—between her legs and making sweet, passionate love to her slightly stubbly mound of Venus with his lips.

But he's a...

Her hips flexed forward. She felt his hand on her

right thigh, lifting it up. She leaned back against the
bench. He pulled back, breathing heavily. His moistened
fingers—first one, then two, gently entered her sacred
chamber, stroking slightly against the inside front. She
moaned, maybe a bit too loudly. Her legs were spread
wide. Her breasts were heaving, still exposed with the
jersey pulled above them. He was looking up at her,
gazing lovingly at her face, examining her in the
moonlight. Her world was swirling. She wanted it to
continue. She loved this. She'd get there. It was on its
way.

Then—without warning—he slowly leaned
forward, and with his flat, gentle tongue, covered her
clit. Gently, he undulated against it, using almost no
pressure at all. He slowly lapped at her. He savored her
while his fingers caressed and rubbed her inside.

Oh my God...He's...He's...

And a vision came back to her: him at that
dance, talking to another parent with his back to her as
she walked in. He turned and recognized her, and she
saw his curly brown hair and wide, generous smile. That

was the moment. That was when she was lost. Now she was in her backyard in the speckled moonlight filtered through the ficus tree, wearing only a sweatshirt, getting her pussy expertly eaten by...this...

"*Ahhhh!*"

White-hot waves washed over her as he rhythmically sucked on her clitoris. Her pussy clamped on his fingers. Her hips tensed and hammered upwards. She heard herself gasping loudly and she drew her hand to her mouth to stifle it. Tightness and shivers covered her body as she felt her clenching around his fingers, which still moved within her. His tongue had turned to fluttering against her clit. Everything was flowing. For a moment, she saw only white. Her molars started to hurt. She lowered her hand to his forehead to tell him it was enough. That would do.

Oh, God, please stop...don't...don't stop.

Her hips jerked upwards once again. And somewhere off in the back of her consciousness, as she floated on a surge of joy, she thought she heard an angel gently strumming a harp somewhere above her.

And as the sensations calmed, with his mouth still planted on her, she felt him softly laugh, and it went through her entire body.

Slowly, he pulled back. He reached up toward her firm breasts, gently touching her nipples. She pulled his hands away. Still too sensitive. She was still coming down. He leaned forward one more time and gently planted an almost-chaste kiss on her mound – one that would have been chaste on almost any other part of her body.

Slowly, he got to his feet. He smiled.

"Thank you," Allie said softly, a slight wobble in her voice. She was still breathing heavily.

"You're welcome," he answered. His voice was low and full, but cheery. She'd heard it under so many circumstances that clashed so entirely with what had just happened. He smiled, nodded, and laughed. He was beautiful. A beautiful man.

"Let me help you with……"

"My pants?"

"Yes." He smiled.

"You must have been looking forward to that, the way you…" She was awkwardly bending down to put her right foot back into her sweatpants.

"Yes, a while. Thought about you all afternoon. All day, in fact."

"I'm glad." He was so beautiful, even now that the prospect of getting back to the real world presented itself and the illusion of a time-outside-of-time receded. The moonlight still had magic.

"You mean even through vespers?" Allie asked. He smiled back.

"Yes, even through vespers. Confession, too."

"It's Friday night. I didn't know there was

confession."

"It was a special appointment. Man with a problem he needed to discuss."

"Oh. I hate those."

"Hate problems?"

"Yes."

"Me too. I try to avoid them. At all costs."

"No, you don't," Allie tittered as she straightened her waistband.

"I mean," he winced for a moment, then returned to his sweet smile. "This doesn't count. What we do doesn't count at all. You are never a problem to me. Never will be."

"We'll see about that."

He took her by the hips and pulled her towards

him. Their gazes intertwined.

"Is there anything I can do to …" She noticed his bulge was still visible.

"To administer to me, you mean?"

"Yes." She almost winced at his choice of words.

"No, not now. I got what I longed for. I'm fine."

"Are you sure?"

"Yes."

She watched as he pulled out his handkerchief and wiped the last of her juices from his chin and lip. Some of her scent remained. He drew the handkerchief to his face and inhaled. She laughed quietly.

"You're going to smell like me all night!"

"I know. It's a reminder of you until we meet

again." He smiled as he put the handkerchief back in his pocket.

"So are we going to see you tomorrow evening?" he asked.

"I hope so. If my mom can take the kids, certainly."

"I hope so, too. You can come to my office. It will need to be tomorrow, or not for a while, sadly. I have business at our mission down in Mexico over next week. Can't put it off any longer, I'm afraid."

Allie would need to make time, then. "In the rectory?" she asked.

"That is where my office is, yes."

Allie looked off back at the house. The beautiful Spanish colonial revival with the tall arches on the patio. The moon was low over it now. It looked like it belonged in some far-flung part of the world—someplace romantic and wild and full of passion.

Someplace that matched the scene that had just unfolded.

"I have a stop to make at the hospital on the way back. I better get going."

"I guess you had better attend to your duties." She smiled as she placed herself against him and stretched. "Father Bernard."

And with another gentle kiss, he squeezed her hand, then walked through the back gate to where his white Chevy Cobalt sedan was parked. He closed the gate, and with one more smile and a wink, he was gone.

Back in bed, Allie reached into her nightstand and pulled out her favourite purple toy. It wasn't very much like him at all, but over the following hour, it stood in for the rest of what she longed for, and what would have made this—their latest encounter—utterly perfect in every way.

3

Rocky Point

D.M. Cobray

Actually, I'm kinda proud of him in a weird way, thought Kristi.

Kristi looked over at Kevin. He had fallen asleep leaning forward in the front passenger seat of the SUV just as they had left Rocky Point on the way back to Scottsdale. He still had Noxzema all over his face, shoulders, and naked, sunburned back. Some of it was had gotten on the leather seat.

Even though he almost did fuck everything up as he usually does…that was…wow …just, wow …

Even with the white crust on his sunburned face, Kevin looked good. Kristi looked up in the rear-view mirror. They looked good together. And in a very legitimate way that mattered to Kristi.

Kevin had started off as arm candy only to have evolved into entertainment, but entertainment mixed with a serious purpose. Kristi's mate needed to be another fit and *dedicated* person—one who looked like a compliment for her. She was a successful entrepreneur. She had far too many events to attend as the "Chief Enthusiasm Officer" behind the RaRaRadish brand and stores she owned, not to mention in her sidelines as an elite yoga instructor and personal trainer. She had a lot of $75 designer headbands and expensive yoga clothes and jewelry to move in her store, and wealthy-though-plump older women to inspire. That made for an exclusive clientele. Having a young guy like Kevin to accompany her was just good business.

Later, she found her son had taken a liking to him as a kind of big brother. So Kevin was in, though there were things about him that irritated her intensely. Meaning: He was about as smart as a bag of hammers.

Nevertheless, the events of the preceding thirty-six hours had inspired new esteem for Kevin in her mind. It was as though she could suddenly respect him in some new way that had nothing to do with his toned pectorals, strong glutes, and curly golden-locks that crowned a baby face.

Maybe I'll keep him, she thought to herself.

But then there was Julio, and there had always been Julio. And there would likely always be Julio– somewhere. Julio was still on her mind. Julio. She looked in the rear view mirror again. She thought back on Julio and the events of the day before. What a scary, intense, yet somehow delightful blast from the past this trip had been. And it wasn't quite over.

About an hour out of town, she slowly pulled up to the border entry station at Sonoyta as she rolled down her window.

"Good afternoon, ma'am. US citizens?" asked the guard as he took their passports. He looked over at Kevin, who still slept, his face slathered in white. Then the guard's mirrored sunglasses lingered on Kristi's tanned thighs. "How many in the back?"

"Two… yes……two." she said, exhaling in

relief as she remembered what had nearly happened. The guard glimpsed at the kids in the back seat, both exhausted, though the boy looked considerably more exhausted and sunburned than the girl. She only looked irritated.

"Drive safely, ma'am," he said as he waved her through. Kristi exhaled deeply.

Scottsdale was a little over three hours away, and although she longed for home, she had strangely mixed emotions. And Julio was in all of them. And she still couldn't quite do it. She couldn't quite let him go. No matter how good Kevin looked, even when he wasn't covered in Noxzema.

* * * * *

It had started out as a normal trip–just a weekend family visit to a friend's beach house. She and the kids were loading luggage and coolers into the back of the Nissan Armada early that Saturday morning as Kevin parked his

Bimmer in front of her nice new stucco house with the Spanish tile. It was a nice scene in a nice, newer neighborhood, and Kevin was a nice guy who looked nice.

"Hey pirate! Hey buddy!" he said as little Braden ran up to him, screaming with glee. Braden loved Kevin. Kelisa, her daughter, tolerated him.

Kelisa was much like her mom: Usually cheerful, but one never knew when she'd drop into that look of cold steel–where nothing mattered but the objective at hand. Braden was a lot more like his father. Kristi loved both of her kids equally, but in Braden, she had never seen that strength of character she secretly admired in herself. It was right under the cheery "Hi, oh hi, how are you??!?! You go girl!!!" hyper-positive attitude she maintained for her customers and clients. She never let the iron beneath show.

Well, almost never.

She had chosen a good-looking joker the first time around in Dave, her children's father. But at least

Dave had the money to pay for his own fun, just as he continued to pay for some of Kristi's and the kids'. Kevin didn't make much money, but he was another good-looking joker. And there he was, letting her eight-year-old son crawl all over him in the front yard: Two of a kind.

Braden ran off to get his new remote-control dune buggy to show to the coolest grown-up in the world. Kevin sauntered up to Kristi and smiled.

"Hey sweetie! I brought along some protection for the trip!" Kevin unzipped his white Adidas jacket and flashed an automatic pistol–a Glock–tucked into his waistband

Kristi was visibly upset, but controlled enough to be sarcastic. "That's great, Kevin. You going to leave it at the border down there?"

"Well, no... I thought we could ..."

Kristi rolled her eyes and gritted her teeth.

"They don't let you take guns into Mexico! Jesus, Kevin, do you know what they'd do to you?" At first she couldn't believe what she had just seen, but then she realized who she was talking to.

"So?" Kevin shrugged. "They don't need to know. I've got some other stuff they don't need to know about either." He winked.

Kristi fumed and yanked him by the arm to the side of the house. They had a long discussion about how he could get not only himself, but also her and the kids thrown into some shitty jail in Sonora after a simple traffic stop once they crossed the border. Sure, he was thirteen years younger than she was, but did that excuse absolute stupidity?

After hiding the gun and Kevin's zip-locked half-ounce of seedy green jankity shit in a cooler in the garage, they all piled into the Armada and headed out of town.

Kevin was a little miffed. He was hoping these buzzkills wouldn't continue. At twenty-seven, he had still never been into Mexico beyond the border town of Nogales, where as an exercise physiology undergrad at University of Arizona, he had experienced his share of wild, drunken Friday nights.

But Kristi had a far different experience of Mexico—one that was far deeper than his. It was something she couldn't share with him, nor with anyone else whom she had allowed into her new life. She had lived through things back when she was Kevin's age— back when Kevin was still a zit-faced kid on a BMX bike trying to shoplift DayQuil. There were things that she still couldn't talk about from those years, and some of them still hurt. As she drove deeper into the Mexican desert, her left shoulder suddenly started aching. She rubbed the scar, the one that the white strap of her halter top barely covered. Her thoughts went back to Julio. She wondered how he was these days.

"Wow, this place looks like...a dump." said Kevin absent-mindedly. He observed the outskirts of Rocky Point through the expensive sunglasses Kristi had bought for him. The roadside was dotted with hand-painted signs offering *mofflers* and *tire-fix* to American visitors. The nicest structures were corrugated prefab buildings. Most looked to be made of cardboard. Stray dogs, goats, and children dotted the side streets of dirt and gravel.

"Be nice."

"I mean, I was expecting something like, you know…Cancun…"

"You've never been to Cancun, either."

"I've seen the pictures."

"It gets better," said Kristi as she admonished him with a slap on his knee.

It's a five-hour drive from Scottsdale to Rocky Point. They call it 'Arizona's beach' for a reason. Many of Christie's customers had condos down there, including the Wagners. It was in Scott and Candice Wagner's condo at the Cabeza Grande that they'd be spending the weekend. Candice Wagner was back in Washington on business–something to do with her work with the SEC and an investigation some kind. They seemed like such a nice couple, and good customers, too. They had two kids of their own, and sometimes they would bring them in to play at the RaRaTorium play discovery area when Kristi brought Braden and Kelisa in after school.

But after what was to happen on this trip, that relationship would need to change, and change radically.

Fifteen minutes of broken pavement and roadside vendors later, the grey Armada nosed into the gated courtyard and past the private security guard– an elderly man with cataracts and a cane. The new condos surrounded the courtyard in shapes resembling a medieval Tuscan castle.

"Damn, this is more like it, Kristi!"

Finally, something to impress Kevin! He jumped out of the SUV as it came to a stop and ran up the flagstone staircase to the large wooden door of one of the units. He started imitating a marching guardsman while saluting, only to lose his flip-flop in the middle of a maneuver. He was such a clown. He made Kristi laugh, and that was important. And Braden loved him. Kristi heard him laughing from the back seat.

It took them about twenty minutes to unload the stuff from the SUV and get everything set up in the condo, which was quite luxurious. Inside, it looked just like Kristi's house in North Scottsdale, with the same black appliances and fake travertine tile and burnt ochre paint. From this viewpoint, Rocky Point seemed like it was just a small outpost of North Scottsdale with a beach. It was a Scottsdale colony.

The kids flicked on the fifty-two inch TV. Braden wanted to watch Transformers, but Kelisa, who was coming into her own at thirteen, wanted to watch a "behind the scenes" VH1 profile of the band Klankenschwetter and their charismatic lead singer, Toby Barrett.

"Mom, it's a rerun! She watches that *all* of the time! It sucks!" whined Braden. Kevin was already trying to mix up some margaritas in the kitchen. He didn't quite know how to put the blender together.

"Shut up, turdcutter," said Kelisa.

"Kids, goddamn it. We are…" Kristi fumed. She stopped herself from flying into yet another tirade. "Who the hell cares! Braden, play with your iPad!" She'd heard something similar from the kids for four hours straight by then. She was done.

Kristi went back to moving organic food from the cooler to the fridge. She turned to Kevin and asked, under her breath, "How quickly can you get me a *fucking* margarita?"

Kevin smiled, embarrassed. He was holding the blender in three separate pieces and looked confused. Kristi brushed past him with a sigh and took over mixing duties.

And so the rest of the afternoon and early evening went, until the kids were in bed.

And then Kristi started to enjoy the fruits of her relationship.

She lay beside Kevin on the leather couch, listening to the waves lapping on the beach outside as the tide rolled in. A *Seinfeld* rerun was playing silently on TV—one they had both seen a few times before, Kristi a few times more than Kevin. Kevin started stroking her sides and flexing his pelvis against hers. He nuzzled her neck delectably as he stroked from her hips to her ribs. His fingers crept up to her still pert B-cups. She felt his thick hardness prodding her in her back. He lowered his shorts and pulled it out, slipping it to rest between her aerobicized buttocks. She moaned a little. This kinda made it all worthwhile—all the juvenile shit she tolerated from him.

"Gonna marry you someday, woman," he said in a bad Ebonic accent. She laughed at his foolishness. "Gots one-a dem *balls* cotched, *woman!* Y'all got me all horny an' sheeit."

Well, that was a little much.

"Kevin, please—shut the fuck up."

"I's jes tryin' to please y'all."

"You know what? Fuck that. You just sound like a racist now." Abruptly, she pulled away from him.

"I'm not, baby."

"You fucking sound like fucking Stepin Fetchit or some shit."

"Who *dat?*" He shook his head and corrected himself. "I mean, *who is that?*"

"Oh shut up, please." Kristi laughed despite herself. "I can't believe I brought *you* to Mexico with me."

Kevin pulled her towards him. She didn't resist much. He moved his head to kiss her. His hand rode up under her RaRaRadish organic bamboo-hemp velour tanktop ($85). She sighed as his strong hand rose up to her breasts, and his fingers drew small, slow, gentle circles around each of her nipples. His tongue darted into her mouth. That's what he was here for. He was a clown. A funny fucking clown. A fucking ...

She felt her bottom involuntarily flexing against him.

Then the door burst open.

Kristi gasped and fell off the couch. Two Mexicans leapt through the doorway. They were both brandishing Uzi submachine guns, one aimed at each of them. Kristi and Kevin put up their hands.

"Dinero! Donde esta el dinero?" The taller of the two demanded. Kevin was hyperventilating.

"Wagner!, Mister Wagner! Where is money?" asked the other one, shaking the gun in Kevin's direction. He seemed like he was just trying to be angry.

"I... I don't know... I..." Kevin was terrified.

Kristi looked up at them, shocked and trembling. *"No somos los Wagner. Estamos usando su propria casa para el fin de semana. Son amigos nuestros."*

The taller guy shook his head. "No, you are from

89

other side. You have money. Wagner."

"No! No somos los Wagner! Permítenos mostrar los pasaportes!"

"No," the guy shook his head and waved his gun. "I know you Wagner."

Kristi silently damned the Wagners and herself for having anything to do with them. They were in the *fucking* drug trade at some level. Kristi knew a thing or two about the drug trade, but only as a fading part of her past. These people were in it up to their arms in the here and now, and they had -- conveniently -- sent her family into harm's way. She tried to imagine how it could be some sort of mistake. It was hard to believe they could have conveniently forgotten about a debt to a Mexican drug cartel before giving them the keys to their vacation condo for the weekend. And it was amazing to think that they both had good positions in the finance business and the government, or at least said they did.

She looked at the two losers in front of her. They were all done up in western shirts and Wranglers and pointy-toed ostrich boots: pudgy minions wearing mustaches. She had memories of these types. They had been brutal fifteen years ago, but generally stayed away from tourist areas like Rocky Point. She glanced at poor Kevin. He was shaking, his hands behind his head, his shorts still slightly askew from their playtime earlier.

The front door creaked open. A middle-aged woman entered. She was short and stout, and in her mid-fifties or so. She had deep-set eyes and a scar on her face that made it look like she had been slashed with a knife across her cheek at some point long before. Her eyes were a deep, dead brown. She walked with a limp, and wore an odd perm that shone with a gloss like Jheri-curl, and was gathered in something like a scrunchie behind her head. She looked like a maid at a Motel 6.

Dispassionately, she looked at Kevin, then at Kristi. "Es problem? Where money?"

"*No tenemos…no somos…* "

"You speak English, lady. I speak English."

"We don't have your money. We don't know anything about it. We aren't the Wagners. We are borrowing their place …" The older woman frowned, shook her head, then nodded at one of the men without letting Kristi finish.

Kristi saw something that made her blood run cold. The shorter of the two henchmen walked past the kitchen and back to the bedroom, back to where Braden and Kelisa were sleeping.

"Wait…" Her heart stopped. "Where is he going? Stop it! *Motherfuckers!*" Kristi tried to rise up from the couch.

Kevin shouted "No!" and grabbed her around the waist, falling to the floor as he tried to restrain her.

Oh my God, they're going to kill my babies!

In a moment, the guy reappeared with Braden in his undershorts. He was holding her panicked little eight-year old by his arm and gesturing towards the front door with the Uzi. Braden's little knees shivered. He frowned, and his lower lip quivered as he looked around him in confusion.

The old woman said something in slang Spanish to the henchman holding Braden.

"It's OK, we take him for now. You get money – fifty thousand– and we give back." She threw down a card with a Mexican phone number etched on it in deliberate strokes with a ball-point pen. "You come with us, little boy. We have fun. Playland. Bye lady."

The henchmen walked little Braden towards the front door. Kristi screamed. As they got him to the transom, he struggled as he reached back to his mother and started to cry. Kristi was on the verge of convulsions. She didn't have fifty thousand available in her cash accounts, and had no way of borrowing it quickly and transferring it to Mexico. If she did, she would have gladly handed it to them right then and there to get her son back.

Kristi felt like she was starting to come apart at the seams, but something deep -- something she hadn't felt in years -- held her together from the inside. She knew she had at least one advantage left. She took a deep breath. She tried to center and focus. Kelisa appeared in the doorway behind the scene. Kristi darted her eyes at her and shook her head.

The woman looked at Kristi but gestured at Kevin. "I have your one son. You go with your other son and find money, OK? OK."

It was bad enough that these thugs were kidnapping her son, but that comment was like twisting the knife. She looked over at Kevin. He was stricken, his whole body shaking as he held his hands above his head.

"OK, and something for you," the woman continued. She reached into the back pocket of her badly fitting, faded jeans and pulled out her nylon wallet. She opened it and flashed a bronze star and an ID card that said "POLICIA". "You don't call police, 'cause I am police, OK? OK."

The three gangsters and Braden disappeared out the front door. It slammed behind them. Kelisa ran out of

the bedroom and into her mother's arms. Kristi hugged
her.

Kristi felt a slight tremble in her spine, then she
felt her back straighten. Her lungs filled with air. She
could handle this. She knew she could. She needed a
little help

"Where did you learn to speak Mexican?" asked
Kevin.

Kristi turned to him slowly, and in slow,
measured tones, she said "Kevin... just shut the fuck
up."

*   *   *   *   *

In the half-hour or so that followed, there was a round of
denunciations, recriminations, and angry rejoinders, and
they all came back to Kevin's condemnations of Kristi
for not letting him bring his gun.

"Kevin, you stupid fucking…where you going to shoot those guys holding the Uzis with your fucking pistol? Is that what you were going to do?"

"A *least* we would have had a chance!"

"No, you would have gotten us and the kids all killed!"

"Now? No: Now it's just your *son!* Your *son* is going to get killed! And probably other things, too!"

"Kevin, please shut the…"

"I will not shut up! *You* shut up! I'm going to go find my little buddy! Whatever it takes!"

"Kevin, don't be stupid! This isn't some stupid fucking Keanu Reeves movie."

"I need to find him. Did you see him looking back? What do you think they're doing with him?"

"Kevin…"

"I will *not* let this happen like this! It *ain't* goin'
down like this, motherfucker!"

"Kevin, I can handle this…I know some
people…"

"I don't want to hear it!"

In a minute, Kevin was in his white Adidas
tracksuit and his matching running shoes. He had his
baseball cap on backwards, in the way he thought meant
business. He grabbed a steak knife out of a drawer in the
kitchen and bounded out the front door. Kristi knew not
where he intended to go and what the later repercussions
might be, but was relieved to get him out of the picture.
He looked back at her once, fire in his eyes. The door
slammed.

"Kelisa, just stay here, OK?"

"OK, Mom."

"Thank you."

*　　　*　　　*　　　*　　　*

Kristi pulled on her RaRaRadish Purple-Nurple hoodie ($115) and a black pair of her SuperLeggara tights ($125) and was out the door. Her iPhone wasn't working. She had forgotten to purchase the card that would allow it to work on Mexican cell networks.

　　　She walked out through the darkness of the courtyard and approached the security guard. He averted his eyes.

　　　"Señor, no ten vergüenza. Los hombres tenían muchas armas." He nodded, then looked up, the emotions of relief and concern showing in his face.

　　　"Señora, discúlpeme… "

　　　"No importa. Conoces a Julio Vargas?"

　　　"Julio Vargas… sí…lo conoces?" he asked with a suddenly stunned expression.

"Sí, lo conozco."

"Sí, sí señora..."

"Llámale ahora, con prisa, porfavor. Es muy importante."

In five minutes, the old man was waving his arm at Kristi, urging her to join him at the wall phone. She rushed over.

"Bueno?"

"Bueno. Is this..." came the groggy voice at the other end of the line.

"Kristi. Remember me?"

"Sirenita..." There was a warmth in his voice that was unmistakable. "How could I forget the Kristi? How are you?"

"I wish I were better, Julio. Someone ..." She almost lost herself. The words came through haltingly.

"Someone…someone has my son."

"No. " His voice was disbelieving and suddenly more alert. "Who?"

"They had Uzis. Cowboy clothes. Looked like Sinaloa. You know guys like that? I haven't seen them in years."

"It's *fucking* Sinaloa." The anger in his voice was palpable. "Kristi, you stay there. Cabeza Grande, right?"

"Yes, the condos."

"I'll be there in ten minutes. Wait… make that fifteen."

"Ok." Said Kristi. The Julio she knew back then would be late to his own funeral. Although she wasn't a praying woman, she prayed to God that he had improved at least a little in the last fourteen years.

*　　*　　*　　*　　*

Fifteen minutes later – on the dot – the gates of the complex opened to reveal a customized orange Chevy Blazer convertible from the early '70s. It pulled into the courtyard. The rumbling V8 engine stopped, and the driver-side door creaked open.

Out stepped Julio Santa Maria Gilberto Sanchez Vargas.

He was every bit the man she remembered. Tall, dark, longish black hair. Black, flashy, expressive eyes. Only some smile lines on his handsome face and a few grey hairs in his eyebrows were there to differentiate him from the image she had of him back when Kristi had been his Girl Friday, his partner, and for a while at least, his presumptive bride.

Overwhelmed with emotion, she ran into his arms.

"Kristi, I am so sorry. "

She couldn't tell him how much she had missed him, at least not right then. He had stayed in shape. She could feel his strong arms and chest.

"I need your help, Julio. "

He listened to the story.

"I know who you are talking about. They're real assholes. *Sinaloense*. They don't know *güeros* from shit. You all look alike to them."

"Well we *are* staying in their condo – the Wagner's, that is."

"You, and?" he asked with a raised brow.

"Well me, and my son and daughter, and my …"

"Husband?"

"No, just a boyfriend."

"Oh." he said, a slight expression of relief

sweeping over his face.

Julio had lived an interesting life. He was born on the streets of Hermosillo and went to a seminary as a twelve-year-old. When his mother died, he crossed the border on foot and ended up graduating high school in Tucson. He made it as far as getting a scholarship to U of A until the lure of the money from smuggling drew him away during the second semester of his sophomore year. When Kristi met him, he was working at a bar in Nogales as a doorman–one who could get you anything you wanted or needed–for a price.

Their relationship had been a tumultuous four years of packaging and selling drugs, running from the cops, and sneaking illegal immigrants over the border and up to Tucson and Phoenix. It had been the richest time in Kristi's life up to that point–both in dollars and in experience–and she could barely imagine her life since without those memories. The years with Julio had made her who she was, even to the point of helping her finance her own apparel and lifestyle company--now worth millions.

"I know where they're holding your son, at least I think I do. They aren't going to hurt him. He's worth way too much to them. Why don't you hop in the truck? We can go and straighten this out."

"My daughter's still in the room," she said. "I don't want to lose her too."

"Don't worry. I'll call my buddy Ephraim. He'll be over in a few minutes to keep his eye on the door."

Kristi held his hand as she pulled away and moved to the passenger side, her eyes locked on his.

He started the Blazer. They rolled away.

"So what's this going to cost me?" she asked.

He turned, looked her in the eye, and smiled out of the corner of his mouth. He made a little shrug.

She knew there was always a price to be paid.

*   *   *   *   *

The sand dunes at the extreme north end of town were isolated and rarely visited, but offered a great view of the sea. The early full-moon rose above the open roof of the Blazer.

They were there on business, but it sure seemed like something else.

After overhearing a phone call in fast and slangy Spanish, Kristi understood the earliest she could expect her son to arrive was by daybreak. The kidnappers needed to make calls on their side – ones to the bosses in Sinaloa. The guys on the ground in Rocky Point were expected to produce income, and they had all written fifty thousand dollars into their plans that would now not be delivered – at least not this weekend.

Kristi's heart ached for her son. She tried to reassure herself. They put him on the phone for a few seconds. He said he was tired but well-treated, and was to sleep in a room with some Mexican kids at a house.

She told him she loved him and that everything would be fine, he echoed back that he loved her, then there was a quick sound of a woman's voice saying "OK? OK." Then the phone went dead.

Kristi and Julio talked about the Sinaloa cartel and how they had branched off from drugs and into protection rackets. Some recent changes in the money pipeline from the US had forced them to collect on debts faster and more ruthlessly. Nevertheless, Julio was convinced that he could get Braden back just after daybreak. They would likely deliver him and just turn him loose, though getting to that point was likely to take a little haggling.

Kristi was about as reassured as she could be, given the circumstances. Now the trick was to wait until daybreak while not going insane.

"Do you know anything about the Wagners?" asked Kristi. "Why would they do this? Send us down here?"

"No, just more Scottsdale people with a condo.

That's all I know. It might not be anything to do with them, really. These *Sinaloenses* just think they smell money, and so they go for it. These Wagners might not be dealing in drugs or anything like it. They just seem rich, so they're targets."

Kristie thought back on what she knew of the Wagners and their lifestyle. They seemed so professional, so buttoned down. Candice was a regulator for the SEC and her husband was a currency trading consultant. They made decent money, but she remembered that both had upgraded from Toyotas to Porsches recently.

"I really find that hard to believe. You and I both know why. Remember the drop we made to that house in Mesa? They were so square they almost looked like Mormons."

"Yes!" Julio laughed. "The baby shower! The one where the gifts had like...what did we do that time? Four kilos maybe?"

"Something like that. I couldn't believe it.

Weirdest baby shower I've ever been to. All those bricks of coke wrapped up so beautifully." She shook her head.

She looked off to the sea and started trembling. She was thinking of what might be happening to her son. She had taken Julio's supposition that killing or hurting a little white kid with rich parents would be a supremely foolish and unlikely thing for even the *Sinaloense* to do. But still, her mind raced.

Julio knew all Kristi could think about was getting Braden back, but he couldn't have her breaking down on the beach until this was over. The exchange was going to be tense enough as it was. He needed to distract her and to keep her distracted.

Kristi and Julio sat on the hood of the Blazer, propped up against the windshield as they looked at the sea, resting on a thick blanket Julio had pulled from under the back seat. They talked about the old times together; the narrow escapes, the weird characters they met, the fights, the second thoughts and brief abandonments, Kristi's wound in the shoulder from that coke-crazed hooker with the .22 in Mazatlan.

"I never thought I'd see you back here," he said.

"I've been back a few times over the years," said Kristi.

"But you never looked me up until now."

"My life's different." A hint of tenderness crept into her voice–as though she wondered what she could still recapture from those wild days.

"Mine's about the same," said Julio, laughing. His hands were folded behind his head.

"I believe it," said Kristi with a smile.

"I haven't changed much. Still just a hustler."

"Like you always were," said Kristi. She knew he was still a hustler in more ways than he ever would admit to her right then, but she didn't care. That was Julio.

"Yeah, more or less," he said with a shrug.

"I hustle yoga pants now," said Kristi with a little sardonic smile.

"Like these?" said Julio, allowing his hand to stroke her thigh.

"Yes ." Kristi smiled. She wondered if she should give in so willingly when her son's life hung in the balance.

She thought to herself that really, there was always a price to be paid. And Julio *was* helping her find her son. There was only a little conflict in her mind that she had to deliberately set aside–something about how it wasn't really a price if she had been willing to grant it to him all along.

"What do they call these?" he asked, gently stroking the fabric of the tight pants covering her hips, allowing the tips of his fingers to linger near her waistline.

She smiled at this amusing opportunity to go into her sales pitch. "Well, I'm glad you asked. These are the RaRaRadish SuperLeggara tights. They're available in a variety of colors. They wick moisture away for a cooling effect, and they're odor-resistant. Did you want a pair for yourself?"

"Well, *Sirenita*," said Julio with a familiar, wry curl to his lips, "I don't remember that odor thing being such a problem with you, but maybe, you know, that that you're older and …" He laughed.

"Oh fuck you, please. You're the one with the fucking smelly feet! Your feet probably still stink like death."

"My feet smell fine, *Sirenita!* Here, smell them." He acted like he was going to lift his foot to her nose.

"Fuck you, you fucking *cholo…*" She pushed his foot away, but in grabbing his ankle, something happened.

She rolled to face him. Their lips met. Her hand raced down his muscled chest. His hand covered her hip, then moved to her ass, sensuously squeezing her. She shuffled in closer to him, inhaling his scent, tasting his tongue. His hand traced a line up her side, lifting her tank top and revealing her breasts and pink nipples. He drew her close to him, panting as their tongues intertwined for the first time in fourteen years.

Kristi reached down and felt his hardness. She had longed for it for almost a lifetime, it seemed. He stretched his pelvis up and allowed her to free his rod from his pants. Her eyes darted at his surging, throbbing member as its moisture glimmered in the moonlight.

Carefully, he returned the favor. Kristi flexed and lifted her hips as he helped her slide the fine fabric of her tights down her legs.

This was so unfair to Kevin, but then, Kevin didn't need to know. Kristi was doing this for her son– for Braden. There was always some price to be paid. Julio didn't owe her a thing. He might have been helping out for old time's sake, but she knew how his mind worked, and she knew how things went down here. Nothing was free, and it all got back to survival. Kristi was doing what she needed to do for her son's survival, and Kevin would just need to understand if he ever found out…if he ever had a chance to find out.

There were so many things on her mind, and yet somehow, the distractions all faded away with the touch of Julio's hot fingers as they gently stroked her naked, wet, yearning sex. He groaned and passionately intertwined his tongue with hers. The truck shook as he peeled off his jeans and unsnapped the last fasteners on his shirt. He was naked in the moonlight. Then, he lifted up her tank top, and she, too, was as bare as nature itself.

"I dreamed about this for so long, Kristi. I wish you'd never left." He kissed her passionately, then allowed his lips to linger on hers softly in a way that had captivated her when they first met all those years ago.

"I never wanted to leave, Julio," she replied softly.

"But you have your life, your family, your job, up in Scottsdale." He drew her closer and pressed his lips against hers again, barely touching.

"I only ever wanted you. I only ever wanted you."

Julio had moved between Kristi's thighs. The moonlight heightened the contrast between her paleness and his darker olive skin. It was a contrast she had missed for years. Firmly and gently he parted her legs, then moved his thick, swollen rod between her lips, teasing her and further moistening the head with each pass. Christie heard herself gasping. This was happening–it really was. The moonlight illuminated his well-muscled chest and shoulders. She squeezed and stroked his upper arms as he moved towards her. There was passion in his eyes and that old smile on his lips. She felt the round head of his rod gently prodding into her hot valley, and they were united again.

Julio pulled grasped her hips and pulled her down towards the edge of the truck's hood to get her away from the windshield. His wonderfully thick cock delved into her wet pussy again. He pressed into her depths. She wanted to give him all. She wanted him to take everything.

"Take me, Julio," she gasped as he thrust into her again and again. She moaned at the pleasure she knew her hot sacred garden was giving his dark cock, and the pleasure he was returning to her with every stroke and lunge. Kristi concentrated on squeezing him with her pussy, tensing as he retreated. Each time she squeezed, his next stroke was harder, faster, and more passionate. It encouraged and inspired him. She was trying her best to milk his hard cock on every stroke. They were already back into their old rhythm. The feel, the sound, the scents were all as she had remembered from years before. She was reunited with the man – perhaps the only man – she had ever really loved.

But in the back of her mind, her thoughts were wrapped around Braden. She already bore so much guilt from the divorce. She had tried everything she could to give him what he needed–though she knew being the only male in a household headed by a hard-charging female entrepreneur made things very difficult on the little guy. This trip was supposed to be an opportunity for her to bond with him, and to let Kevin bond with him in the way she wished her ex-husband could have – had he not fully lost himself in booze and drugs and his own hidden sadness before he dealt himself out of their lives.

She deeply wished it had been some other occasion to reunite her with Julio. How many times had she been tempted to drop everything and come down to see him on a weekend? How many other trips to Rocky Point had she spent wondering where he was and what he was doing, and if he still prized her?

But now he was pulsing deeply within her again, reminding her of the four years when their souls intertwined at every opportunity – in vans, in cheap hotel rooms, on deserted roadsides in remote parts of Arizona and New Mexico, and on beaches just like this one up and down the Sea of Cortez. She began to feel the deep, ravishing hunger he aroused in her. She hadn't felt it since the days when the world was theirs and fate seemed only one misstep away, an abiding presence of danger that told them to live, just live their lives in the present as intensely as they possibly could.

She pressed at his right shoulder. He knew what that meant. He still remembered.

Carefully, he twisted himself to her side. He used to be able to do this without pulling out, but he had lost some coordination–and they *were* both were on top of a Blazer's hood, after all. They both laughed as his length popped out. He rolled on his back and scooted himself closer to the windshield. Kristi lifted herself up on her hands and knees, and then carefully straddled him. She was feeling a deep, familiar hunger. She reached down and aligned him with her core, and slowly slid down onto his hot, hard shaft. He gasped and moaned. She shuddered. She enveloped him in her hot tightness while using her muscles to grasp and massage him. And then the grinding started.

She rubbed herself against him and felt the pressure on her as she started her deep grind. He looked up into her eyes, flexing his hips to meet hers. *This* is how she remembered them relating. *This* was how they would show love. *This* is how they would communicate things that words couldn't express. *This* was how they would settle differences. Carefully, she moved her feet under her. All that training and yoga had helped her maintain her limberness all these years. She moved to a deep squat and bounced on him, flexing her inner muscles at the bottom of every stroke. His eyes widened in the moonlight as he moaned. His hands guided her hips. As she felt his body tensing beneath her, she arched her back and lifted her head up towards the stars – moaning, then almost shouting with pleasure.

Kristi felt her surge of warmth starting in her core and racing up the the center of her body to the top of her skull. From beneath her, Julio pumped harder and harder, faster and faster as he slammed up against her, deeper and ever deeper into her wet and grasping vice.

"Kristi…Kirsti… baby… *te quiero!"* Julio roared as he came, spilling his warm jets of cream into her depths. She fell forward and grasped his shoulders, grinding hard against him one last time, and then her own orgasm overtook her, raging with searing intensity through her entire body.

*   *   *   *   *

At some point, Julio passed out on the hood. Kristi got

dressed and lay next to him, staring at the moon and hoping that Braden was in good hands. At least she felt satisfied that she had done what she could to ensure his safe return as far as Julio was concerned. She couldn't sleep. The waves played their music, but it was no consolation to her.

When Julio groaned himself awake, it was near sunrise. The rosy-fingered dawn had just begun to tease the horizon behind them. Kristi looked both up and down the beach for any indication that those criminals were bringing Braden back. In desperation, she lowered herself to the ground. Tensely she paced back and forth in the sand, counting her steps. She felt the grains against the soles of her feet and between her toes.

One… two……three…. She looked out towards the Sea of Cortez. It looked beautiful, especially at this hour. But under the surface, she knew it was contaminated and full of filth. Her mind raced back to the look on that woman's face as she gestured for her henchman to seize her son. A white-hot streak of rage went through Kristi's body. She started running back towards town.

Julio jumped to the ground, pulled on his shorts and ran after her.

"Kristi, wait! We need to wait here!"

"It's daybreak! They said daybreak! I want my fucking son back!" she yelled back over her shoulder.

"Kristi, you gotta give them a chance! Let's call them!"

"No, they have *had* their chance! I want my son! They aren't going to let him…"

She felt his hands on her shoulders. He touched her scar. It stung. She leapt around to face him, sneering and lashing out, seething. He grabbed her by the arms and yanked her to him. His hand came back for a second as he snarled.

"What are you going to do, Julio?" she shouted, a tremor in her voice. "*What are you going to do?* Is it going to be like that time in Juarez?"

He stared into her eyes, then gently, slowly pulled her towards him. Her arms went around him. His hand stroked her back, and they kissed again. In a moment, their pants were off and she was on her back in the sand.

Back at the truck, Julio made another call to the kidnappers.

Kristi sat in the Blazer, softly whispering self-affirmations while Julio gently rubbed her arm and stroked her thighs. Every ten or fifteen minutes brought another phone call or attempt to connect somehow as the sun rose above them. It was draining and infuriating to Kristi, but Julio gave her reason to hope. He reminded her of how things worked down in Mexico, and that they usually – *usually* – had come out for the best. It just took time and patience.

Kristi tried her best not to nurse a hatred for the Wagners. She wanted to believe it was all a mistake and a misunderstanding. She just didn't know how that could be.

The story behind the negotiations on the other end of the calls kept changing, and Julio responded with his offers of substitutions for Braden. He profiled Kristi and her older son Kevin as poor people from West Phoenix who were borrowing a friend's condo and didn't have $50,000 nor even $500 to their names, his promises of consequences if the kid wasn't returned safely and soon, and so on.

Finally as the sun was well past its midpoint in the sky, the negotiations came down to $500 in ransom, which Julio himself offered to pay at some undetermined point in the future. Finally, a delivery time was set half an hour from then – which likely meant something more like an hour.

Kristi was sick of this shit. She wanted her son back. She wanted to be home. She wanted to know Kevin was all right. What's more, her gut was grinding in hunger. She wanted a shower. She still had sand in uncomfortable places from the last time with Julio. She had been doing some basic yoga poses on the beach and meditating. When she'd flex, she'd feel Julio's eyes upon her. He wasn't getting that again, yet–at least not just now.

Finally, an old red Chevy Suburban with custom chrome rims trundled over the dunes behind them. Kristi leapt in excitement as she looked through the windshield to see three adults: two in the front and one in the back. As it got closer, she recognized the older lady in the passenger seat. The truck revved and drove past the Blazer, parking at a distance of about a half-block further down the beach. Julio moved to the back of the Blazer and signalled Kristi to move as well. He dropped the tailgate.

It took all she had in her to keep from running to meet the Suburban and yanking the door open. These *pendejos* had fucked with the momma bear.

The passenger-side door opened on the Suburban. One of the men from the night before stepped out, an Uzi still slung around his neck. He walked across the beach to meet Kristi and Julio. He nodded as he approached. Julio nodded back as he stepped out to meet him, signalling Kristi to say put.

"We have boy, Miss Wagner," he shouted past Julio.

"*Cabrón, ya te dije, ella no es la señora Wagner*" said Julio.

"*No importa. Ella es del otro lado, cabrón. Si conocen los Wagner, me imagino que son ricos.*"

"*No tienen nada, ella es simplemente una maestra,*" said Julio simply.

"*Sus pantalones, son de RaRaRadish. Yo se que son muy caros, cabrón.*"

Julio just shrugged and silently wondered what the hell was happening to the world when a low-level *Sinaloense* minion knew the street value of yoga pants and judged the wearer accordingly.

Kristi looked past the Blazer and up the beach at the Suburban. Her heart leapt as she noticed the silhouette of a small head moving behind the tinted windows. Braden was with them. Now if they could just get this fucking *negocio* behind them.

"I think if you give me five hundred now, I think is all right," said the guy to Kristi.

"She doesn't have five hundred. I'll give you five hundred. But not now. *Mas tarde*," snapped Julio.

The guy looked off in the distance for a moment and shrugged, then turned around and walked back to the Suburban.

"I think they'll bring him now," said Julio to Kristi, softly.

Sure enough, the back door of the Suburban opened and Braden popped out. He started running towards his mother. Her heart leapt, but then the two men grabbed him by the arms and started walking him across the beach towards where Kristi and Julio were parked.

Julio looked perturbed. Were they still going to try to get money out of him? Money he didn't have?

"*Putamadre,* " he said under his breath. This was just more bullshit to be waited out. Give them five more minutes of talking and standing around and they'd get bored and leave the kid. Even they knew how stupid this all was, but they had numbers to make.

But then as they had marched the frightened boy with the sunburned cheeks almost halfway to the Blazer, something remarkable happened.

Out of the wild shrubs near the beach sprang a vision. It was partially dressed in white. It appeared to be wearing long white pants and to have a sort of white headdress on. The phantom came charging out from behind a shrub, arms flailing above its white-clad head.

"*Let go of Braden you fucking assholes!*" screamed the creature in a voice that sounded very familiar to Kristi. The two men let go of Braden, then turned their Uzis towards the creature. Bullets flew in all directions. Kristi screamed and ran from behind the Blazer, charging towards Braden. Braden stood with his hands covering his ears, then deliberately threw himself on the ground in a way he had seen his heroes on TV do.

Julio reached inside the Blazer and grabbed something from beneath the back seat. He ran to catch Kristi. He knocked her down to the sand from behind. She screamed as a couple of nine-millimeter rounds from one of the Uzis hit the beach near her head. Julio ran past her towards the scene with a combat shotgun, a menacing black creation with rails and handles all over it. The men with the Uzis were firing blasts of lead, but they weren't hitting anything, terrified as they were at the pale menace thrashing before them with a steak knife in his hand and his jacket on his head. They both staggered clumsily on the beach in their boots.

"*Orale, pendejos! A Sinaloa, putos!*" shouted Julio as he fired two rounds from the shotgun. It was only loaded with birdshot, but that was enough.

In a hail of birdshot, the men with the Uzis – now with empty magazines – ran in their pointy ostrich-leather boots to the Suburban and stumbled inside. The pudgy woman behind the wheel revved the engine and they were off, swearing and waving their guns through the window as all four tires kicked up rooster tails of sand.

Kristi finally let herself cry as she embraced Braden. He was sunburned from playing outside with kids at the safehouse where they had kept him, but seemed otherwise OK. He even had a pair of cargo shorts and a faded "Bimbo" soccer jersey that he wasn't wearing when he had been seized. Kristi held him and they both cried, though Braden was anxious to show the Spanish he had picked up during his imprisonment.

"*Pinche verga!* Mom! *Pinche verga!*" Kristi smiled, then calmly told him in Spanish, then again in English, that he was never, ever to use that phrase again under any circumstances.

Julio drove everyone back to the Cabeza Grande. They stopped at the on-site clinic and had Kevin and Braden checked over by a nurse. With the exception of some small cuts and bruises sustained while playing rough, he was fine and in good spirits. Kristi cringed when he asked if he could go back and play at the house with the Mexican kids again.

Kevin was in worse shape, having taken his jacket off at some point and wrapping it around his head while on the hunt for Braden. He had met up with an American priest who gave him hints on where to find a kidnapping victim. He had staked out the safe house then had hired a cabbie to tail the Suburban after seeing Braden getting loaded into it. Kevin was as red as a lobster.

Kelisa had spent the whole time drawing a portrait of Toby Barrett from Klankenshwetter on her iPad and didn't notice they had been gone so long.

Kevin thanked Julio profusely with a strong handshake. Julio accepted it with a gracious smile and shrug while looking over Kevin's roasted shoulder at Kristi, who shyly diverted her eyes. Julio introduced his friend Ephraim, still there to protect the family from any reprisals from the Sinaloa gangsters. Ephraim stood about six-foot three and wore a jean jacket he couldn't quite get closed.

Kristi looked at her reunited family, and then back at Julio.

"Kevin, why don't you and Ephraim take

Braden and Kelisa down to the hotel store and get some ice cream and Noxzema for your burns, hon? I want to talk a bit more with Julio about the Wagners and what to do about that." She reached into her phone case and pulled out a $50 bill and pressed it into his hand. She leaned forward to kiss him, being careful not to touch his burns.

With the door shut behind her, she turned to look at Julio.

"I want to apologize for freaking out at you and being a pain earlier."

He shook his head. "Your son was kidnapped. I understand. I'm just glad he got back."

"Like you knew he would."

"Yeah, I thought it was going to be ok."

"And I'm sorry for what Kevin did. I know it complicates things."

Julio inhaled deeply, then shrugged with a smile. "I'll live...I'm pretty sure. But you're right, it kinda complicates life here. The *Sinaloense* don't like anything that looks like competition."

"I know. I am really sorry." Kristi leaned forward and took his hands in hers, smiling. "How else can I make it up to you?"

Julio smiled in his infinite charm. He looked into her eyes. His fingers gently rose to her lips and traced them.

"I've been wanting your lips for so long, Kristi." She smiled. His touch once again set her aflame.

She felt him through his pants, then undid his belt. She yanked his jeans down and freed his rod yet again. It was already half-hard and was almost springing to its full, impressive length and girth. Its darkness delighted her. Her tongue raced to meet the head. She looked up at him as her tongue traced lines around the crown and underside of his cock. She lapped at the sweet pre-cum that had already accumulated near the tip. He was so hot. She felt him pulsing against her tongue as she took him into her mouth. He had a spice to the way he tasted that delighted and excited her. Her hand curled under his heavy balls and caressed them as he moaned.

He was overcome with sensation and started prodding into her mouth almost uncontrollably. He was saying "Yes, yes, yes" in between gasps. She squeezed his shaft with her hand to control his depth and give him more pleasure. He was straining and moaning as he pressed deeper into her mouth. She sucked on his head, pressing the lips he admired so much just behind the ridge behind the crown. She was reminded of how much she loved doing this with him.

But he was getting close, and she could sense it. She had other things in mind for this time.

She pulled back and looked up at Julio. There was urgency in her voice. "I want you. Fuck me."

Julio reached down and pulled her to her feet. He bent her over the couch and yanked down her pants. This time he was a little more rough, perhaps even dominant. But his cock sweetly pressed into her, and he ran his hands up and down her sides, pausing to squeeze her hips expressively as he dwelled inside of her with every stroke. After what seemed like a blessed eternity, she felt her orgasm rising up. He started to get more intense, slamming into her, harder and faster as she convulsed. No sooner had one wave ended that another took her, then another, and yet another still. And finally with Julio gasping with everything he had and almost shouting he flooded her yet again with life.

They both collapsed on the sofa. After a minute or two of deep and heavy breathing, Kristi turned towards him. "Julio?" she asked.

"Yes?"

"I have an idea of how we might be able to help each other."

*   *   *   *   *

By nine AM the next day, the SUV was loaded again

and they were ready to go.

Kristi loaded it herself after telling Kevin that he had better not strain himself after his severe sunburn. He sat inside the condo and watched TV with the kids. Soon enough, the family was together in the Armada and on their way back home, northbound out of Rocky Point.

Kristi felt blessed to be reunited with her son, and was still oddly impressed by Kevin's crazy, foolish, and unwarranted charge to the rescue.

But she was half-hearted about needing to return to her legitimate life in North Scottsdale and her impending confrontation with the Wagners.

Because, just... well... wow... just ... wow.

4

Ashley Roarke Must Have Sex (Or She Will Die)

D.M. Cobray

Ashley felt a mix of disappointment, disgust, and desperation that Sunday afternoon. That mixture had become all too familiar to her. It was gravely serious and threatening.

Her lover had gone soft again. He groaned as he rolled over, pushing her off of him as he did. His face was buried in his own arm. Most guys his age should have been good for three goes in ninety minutes or so. He had barely finished one, and a second looked like it wasn't going to happen–at least not right then. What's more – it didn't seem that it was worth waiting on him to recover.

She looked over his smooth, muscled back and ass, still sweaty from his glorious-to-him three and a half minutes or so of exertion. His balls were peeking out from between his legs. He was cute, but couldn't deliver what she needed. He groaned again.

At least Ashley had managed to have an orgasm from it–a brief, almost polite one. It was enough to stave off her demise for a little while, at least. But she knew she needed more. She knew from past experience that she only had a few hours left, and then the inevitable would happen. She was in the middle of a bad episode— an especially bad one.

They varied in intensity, these episodes. Sometimes they would show up as a little reminder—a little pang somewhere in her body. That gave her time to try to find someone new or to contact one of her favorites—one who hadn't been run off or married or something else yet. For those, she could take her time and do it right, and usually she was OK for a week or sometimes even a month. But there was something intense about this one—something that reminded her of the last time she had been hospitalized and had barely gotten out alive. She couldn't go back there.

She looked at her hands and her wrists. She

wondered what made it worth it. What made her go on like this? There had to be a simpler way. Some way out. She had thought about it so many times over the last two years. Life wasn't supposed to be like this. It didn't need to be like this.

But like this, it was.

She looked over at him. He was so young and conventional, with his gym body and his white USC cap lying to his side. How could she tell him the truth? Could he even come close to understanding? Would he even care? No one had, yet. Not a single one. No one she told about her problem could understand, nor help her, beyond the occasional treatment.

Ashley felt a flutter in her lower abdomen and near the tops of her inner thighs. She looked down at her body and hated herself again. What had she done to deserve this? Why had nature betrayed her? Why were these things that were so simple for millions or even billions of others so difficult for her?

But she wasn't one to dwell on these things.

Dwelling on it hadn't helped the first year after her diagnosis. In the second year, she had learned to deal with it more effectively. She had learned to deliberately, forcefully put suicide out of her mind. Something would get better. Something had to come along. Just because it… well, it just had to. Hope was all she had.

But now she was back on the bed in her apartment. She had needs, very specific ones. She looked at the boy beside her. She didn't think of him as a man. He hadn't been enough. He hadn't moved with desire.

She needed another one. Another good one, one who understood how to do it. If she couldn't get it, she knew the pain was going to come, and after the pain the numbness, then her breathing would become sporadic, then someone—maybe her latest lay (was it Cory or Cody? She couldn't quite remember)—would get concerned and call 911. The paramedics would come and put her on an IV, defibrillate her, put her on a respirator mask, shoot her up with all sorts of things to get her to start breathing again and her heart beating on the way to the emergency room. And there would be

EKG's and x-rays and MRIs and more and more drugs as her biological existence continued its downward spiral. And all of these heroic efforts—the best modern medicine could deliver–would take her further away from the one thing that could sustain her life.

She needed to have sex – strong, vigorous sex – with a man, or else she would die. It was a matter of life or death. And it seemed no one else could understand. She lay in bed next to Cory or Cody or whomever. He had started to snore now. He had been a disappointment—but really, no worse than a lot of others.

He had swaggered up to her at the Laundromat at the apartment complex in the same way many men did. They were generally pretty alike.

Oh hey, you work out? Yeah, me too. I bench in the four hundred-range. Yeah.

That was bullshit, but he was cute. What was more important was that he was young, and his strong-looking glutes made Ashley think he could go all night.

141

She had envisioned him on top furiously pumping as he channeled the power of creation into her, allowing her to return to a full physical existence.

So hey, you like Klankenshwetter? Yeah, I got their album. I know Toby Barrett personally. Met him a couple times. Yeah, he's a really cool guy.

He had gone on about whatever. It was shit boys his age said to girls his age. It didn't work on them either, much less thirty-two year olds. But Ashley really didn't need to hear it. She felt her heat and wetness surging in her center as she stood there near the washer, bra in her hands. Cory or Cody would do nicely, she thought – and he had just walked up to her.

Facing him, she slowly approached. She looked him in the eye. She reached forward and felt him through his loose gym shorts. He had a good flaccid size. She felt a wave of energy course through her, even more as she looked into his eyes and saw a brief moment of terror come over him. He looked at the other side of the room, near where an old Mexican woman was tending to her second load. He stifled a laugh. Then she felt him getting hard.

So, uhh, did you wanna go out? Meet up some place and hang out?

He was clueless. He didn't know this wasn't really fun for her. She had long given up on the idea of courtship and anything like a relationship. When she ran into this sort of thing, she would sometimes feel like crying. She felt like asking these guys, "Do you not understand that if I don't get this I will die?" But that would just scare them off. Talk about red flags!

"I need your cock." Ashley heard these soft, breathy words come through her throat, spirited up from some gravelly place in her soul. "I need your cock in my pussy."

She could almost tell his knees were wobbling as they stumbled off side-by-side to her second-floor apartment near the pool. She slammed the door behind them. She dropped her sweatpants and pulled him towards her, yanking down his shorts and going down on him in a singular motion. He was still hard at that point.

143

That had happened about fifteen minutes ago. And now, after a few dozen strokes and a hand-finish all over her back, he was done. Snoring. He had a nice red Corvette and not enough fuel to make it run. Later that night, he'd probably tell his friends how he had "destroyed some MILF pussy" earlier that day.

Yeah, right. Whatever.

She looked down at her mound and stroked and squeezed it. Toys weren't going to do it. Fingers couldn't provide what she needed.

She needed a man driven by desire.

She needed her hair pulled and to feel his hips slamming up against hers as he squeezed her and rammed into her wet, grasping pussy with a manic energy, bounding into her depths like he wanted to fill her with a thick, heavily-veined cock. She needed to hear him shouting at her in raucous, growling syllables that meant nothing but "*fuck*". She needed to shout back at him, groaning and screaming as some eternal energy filled her and animated her entire core from her vagina

144

to the top of her head, emerging almost literally in a shower of sparks. It needed to be rough, direct, immediate. And she needed it to last long enough for her to get up on her plateau, the wondrous dimension, the land of the perfection of the animal spirits: the Lovely Land of Orgasmia.

And she needed it to happen that day, as soon as possible. Then, she knew she could live.

If she didn't find it, she knew she would die. The doctors had told her, and previous experience had (almost) proven it.

As she lay there, she sensed the veil of darkness descending upon her as the first sign of arrhythmic breathing hit. The wet blanket was rolling over her. It had already started.

"Hey. You're done. I gotta do something else." She slapped Cory or Cody on his ass and nudged him. He grunted and shook off his stupor as he started gathering his clothes. Ashley carefully got up and went to the shower.

Through the steam, somewhere in the background, she could hear him saying, "Hey thanks, I'll call you," or some drivel as the front door slammed.

It was 1:30 on Sunday afternoon. Based on what she remembered from her last serious bout, she estimated she had only about four hours left.

*   *   *   *   *

What a peculiar life Ashley had lived for the last two years. The things she had to do just to survive. She looked into the mirror as she dried her hair.

Her sorry state was the last thing she would have imagined as a kid. In childhood and adolescence, she had always been the one left watching TV or reading by herself while her sister and her friends played doctor or spin-the-bottle or made out. It would gross her out, watching what they did. Her mom always looked at Ashley as the responsible one—her little angel. Her father generally left parenting to Mom, but Ashley remembered him being affectionate and loving before he'd died back in her childhood. Mom didn't talk about him much. She was a sensitive soul, and his passing still hurt.

She didn't even get kissed until she was almost nineteen. That was when her boss at BurgerShack cornered her in the office after-hours. He was a man twice her age, awkward, stumbling, balding, and portly. And all she could remember was that despite his gut, his moustache, the smell of grease on his face, and the pictures of his eight half-Hispanic kids on the office wall behind her, her toes were twinkling as she walked out to her Corolla that night, almost in spite of her basic revulsion.

It was only a kiss, but it was her first. Finally, she had felt the desire of another for her.

Through college and her first few jobs afterwards, and even her first few years after attaining her dream job at HammerCo Investments, she had tried to stay away from the meaningless non-relationships she saw her friends dive into with a relish. There would be

147

no easy hook-ups for Ashley Roarke. There had to be something better—something greater out there for her. It was too bad she wasn't going to find it as a math major, nor in the audit department of a financial services company. She couldn't see the men who surrounded her as eligible in the least. So she went without, and with the exception of that one guy she met on vacation in Mazatlan when she had finally lost her virginity, she had dates with her vibrator.

She looked herself over in the mirror. She had a filled out nicely at some time in the past, and her figure showed its prime condition at thirty-two years in the way that everyone seemed to like. Her longish, curly red hair spilled over her softly freckled shoulders. She beheld herself, drops of water still dewing her full breasts. She struck a pose, tilting her hips in a way that she thought looked hot.

Why was it so impossible to find even just one guy who could do what she wanted, give her what she needed in order to survive? What was wrong with her?

Doctor Vincanti had known what was wrong

with her, and he had told her. Most people still refused to believe it really was a problem. Their dismissiveness depressed and enraged her. They didn't understand.

Just as she reached her thirtieth birthday, there were days when she'd awaken and find herself unable to get out of bed right away. At first these just seemed like bouts of depression based on her fear of aging. She started a round of Welbutrin and tried to get on with life. After three weeks, not much had changed. She couldn't breathe at times. Her heart rate was irregular. She'd wake up with fluid in her lungs as though she were suffering heart failure.

Finally, she came home from work one day and couldn't get up the short staircase to her apartment. With her heart palpitating and her cheeks flushed, she lay on the staircase, trying desperately not to tumble down. She cried out. The retired lady next door found her and called 911.

She spent a week at Desert Regional Medical Center on a respirator, undergoing tests. Her sweet and loving mother sat by her side through it all, having dropped everything and driven in from Fresno as soon as she heard.

On day seven her doctor somberly walked in the room. After exchanging niceties, he politely asked her mother to leave them in privacy. She complied, but very reluctantly. The doctor made sure the door was closed behind her.

"I have been investigating your case, young lady," said Doctor Vincanti, a somewhat handsome blonde internist of about forty-five or so. He had a wry expression on his face, only slightly offset by an abiding sense of grim strangeness at what he had to communicate.

"You seem to have a very unique set of circumstances. It's not just hormonal. It seems to be in your nervous system as well. There are a few such cases on record. Your autonomic processes—like your breathing and cardiac function—need to be excited through a very specific means..."

"Like what, doctor?"

"A very specific sort of...stimulation..."

"Like what?" she asked, terror seeping up her spine.

"Well..."

When she finally heard what the specific means of stimulation was—the doctor's prescription after a week of studying case histories and consulting with neurologists and endocrinologists—she burst into tears. She nearly ripped out the IV and heart monitor and crawled out on her own.

Here she was, barely able to move and this, this *doctor* –- this *pervert* — was trying to fuck her. He probably would have tried to do her right there in the hospital room with her mother outside the door. She cried, panicked, and rolled over and hit the nurse call button. The nurse and her mother rushed into the room, and the doctor excused himself, embarrassed.

Later that afternoon, she was discharged at her own request.

As she spent the evening of her release in her living room surrounded by her cats, stuffed animals, and chicken soup, floating on a cocktail of anti-depressants, Lasix, and amphetamine salts, her mother wondered why she wouldn't tell her specifically what the doctor said to her. She sat and watched a *Seinfeld* marathon on TV. She had seen most of them before.

But as she sat there in her semi-delirious funk, Ashley started thinking about something else. At first it nauseated her. She started thinking about her manager at BurgerShack all those years ago. She started thinking about what else could have happened when he took her by her shoulders and pressed her against that wall.

Despite herself, she started imagining his thick fingers probing her tight, wet, virgin quim – at first through the polyester fabric of her uniform pants, and then directly as his hand slid down inside the waistband of her panties.

"Mom, could you get me some soda? At the store?"

"We have Sprite, honey."

"I know, but...but...I really need 7Up."

"Uhhh... well, OK, sweetie." Mom put on her shoes, grabbed the keys and was off. Ashley was so lucky to have a wonderful mother like hers, she thought.

After she heard the car starting outside, her hand went down to her mound, and then under her pajama bottoms. She didn't like what was going through her mind, but her thoughts just kept going back to her manager. At a certain level she despised him. He was gross and had cornered her and made her feel cheap and helpless. She had quit shortly after the incident, which she'd never confessed to anyone.

But it was desire. It was movement and energy. It was a man just being a raw, coarse, irresponsible male – damn his family obligations and corporate HR rules and the threat of litigation and a criminal complaint. He was motivated by overwhelming desire, a wave of some eternal, universal flow of energy that had risen up and caused him to urgently press himself against her lips.

Yet despite everything that was wrong with it, with her aching legs spread, she brought herself to orgasm thinking about that heavy-set forty-two-year-old man helping her out of her polyester uniform pants, laying her little nineteen- year-old frame on his desk and prodding her with his hard cock, which in her imagination was thick and long enough to extend beyond his turgid belly. She didn't love him. She didn't want him physically. He was disgusting. But she wanted to surrender to his cock. She needed him inside of her. There was something so powerful in that memory from all those years ago. She flexed and bounced her hips as she felt a tingling start, and as the waves of pleasure overtook her, the memory of the manager's face faded and she felt the curtain lift from her body, if only for a moment.

When the orgasm from her fingers subsided, the heavy curtain slowly started to come down again – a bit more lightly this time. She still wanted more. She needed more.

The next day she called the doctor's office and told him she needed to see him right away. Her mother helped her get dressed. She was feeling a little better, thanks to her energy burst from the night before, but she didn't trust herself to drive. She asked her mother to wait in the car, but she insisted on coming into the waiting room. Ashley's legs were shaking. She walked into the office, short of breath. In the exam room, the nurse helped her out of her clothes and into a surgical gown, and she waited on the table.

"How are you feeling, Ashley?" asked the doctor in a soft, therapeutic tone as he quietly entered. A stethoscope was slung around his neck.

She looked at him as though he were bringing water to her on a desert island. She felt her shoulders heaving and a fluttering in her belly. The door closed. She got to her feet and staggered to him, lifting up her surgical gown to reveal herself. She wrapped herself around the doctor. Startled, he tried to move back. With him up against the wall, her hands moved down between his open white coat, and she felt ...

Nothing.

"Ashley, please...you've gotten the wrong impression. Please, sit down."

Her disappointment was overwhelming.

"But, I...I thought ..."

"You thought I was just trying to get you into bed? Is that what you thought, Ashley?"

"I suppose, yes...but ..."

"Now you're feeling the urge, right? The bad feeling is on you and you want for the entire world to get it off of you? Right? And now you know what you need."

"Doctor, I can't breathe ..."

"I know."

"Please *help me*!"

"I can't."

"I know you can! You admitted you could!" said
Ashley. She slowly, achingly spread her legs on the
exam table in a way she hoped he'd find overpowering.

"I never said I could help you in that way,
Ashley."

"But it's obvious you …"

"Ashley, I'm gay."

That told her everything she needed to know.

It was real: She was really ill. And it seemed
there was only one thing that could possibly cure her or
even allow her to go on living.

The rest of the visit consisted in the doctor
helping her back into her clothes as he advised her on
safe sex practices, prescribed birth control, and educated
her on the strange nature of her particular ailment, the
exceedingly rare *Bonaparte Syndrome*.

On the tearful way home from that visit, she still

avoided telling her mother what the doctor had
determined. She told her only that they had done more
tests and were waiting on results. She sure as hell wasn't
going tell her about her behavior in the exam room.

When she got home from that visit to the doctor,
barely breathing and crying with dismay at what had
suddenly become of her life, her mother helped her sit
down in front of the TV in the recliner and handed her
the laptop computer she had requested.

Her mom watched Ashley and cooed at her in
sympathy as she got settled on the couch. When Ashley
was fairly certain her mom's attention was focused on
the TV and not on her, she created an account on
DatingPalmSprings.com. She had resisted doing
anything with online dating so far in life. This counted
as a desperate measure.

After putting in all of her information and
determining which picture to use, a few dozen guys
immediately hit her up. They all looked either dangerous
or ugly or old. Then, she realized that she was a barely-
mobile sick woman in an apartment, tended to by her

mother and her two cats. And she started to cry.

The next day her mother had to meet someone in Sacramento in regards to her own disability claims for her injured back. She joked that they made quite the pair. She made sure Ashley had what she needed and could move around and could call on the neighbor lady. She left Ashley to her own devices with a promise that she could come back with a single call to her cellphone if it proved necessary. Ashley hugged her and thanked her. It was so good having a mom like her.

As soon as the door shut, Ashley went to the kitchen and pulled out the garbage can from beneath the sink. She took it back to the living room and – with some strain – lifted the silk palm from its large, shiny plastic pot. She overturned the garbage into the pot. And there, at the top of the pile liberated from the kitchen garbage, was a number written on a cocktail napkin. A guy had pressed it into her line of sight on the bar when she was at happy hour at the Purple Room with her coworkers about ten nights before, just before she started feeling ill. She barely remembered him. The napkin was stained with coffee grounds.

An hour later, she was limp and leaned over the back of her sofa as her cats Moco and Zippy watched her getting plowed from behind by Raymond. He wasn't that young and wasn't that attractive and was probably married, but was willing. And hard.

He fucked her on the couch to a decent orgasm, and then, with some of her strength restored, she rode him cowgirl-style as he lay on the carpet in front of the TV, her movements and sounds getting more and more giddy as her second orgasm approached. Shortly after she finished, he was called away by a text on his cellphone that made him blush and act flustered and awkward.

Ashley showered, then slept soundly. At the sound of the alarm the next day, she nearly bounded out of bed. She was well again, and her mother was delighted by her miraculous recovery. Her mother even called the doctor to thank him for whatever he did to cure her. He only answered, "You're very welcome. Please be gentle and understanding with your daughter." She didn't understand what he meant.

Raymond called and texted a few times after that, but she wouldn't answer. She was done with him. Everything was fine again. *Thanks. Go back to your wife!* Ashley didn't know that this aching need would be a frequent occurrence, nor how severe it would be. Everything seemed fine.

And everything *was* fine again. For a while.

*   *   *   *   *

That had been two years ago; two years and an unknown number of fuck partners ago—most of them anonymous. And as she applied some lipstick and mascara all she could think about was how little she could have predicted about her life based on that one visit to Doctor Vincanti back then.

Her ailment – and its treatment – had led her in some interesting directions.

She slipped into her brown wraparound dress—

the one that looked like a Halston original from 1977. She didn't bother with a bra or panties. She strapped on some casual heels and walked down to her Prius. It was a hot August day in Palm Springs, but there had to be some men out and about somewhere.

As she drove along, she saw men in cars and trucks going in the opposite direction. Any one of them would do. Or rather, anyone could do, potentially. She yearned for each of them, but especially the harder-looking ones who made a living pouring concrete or hammering nails or laying bricks. And whenever someone on a Harley would pass in the opposite direction—its loud exhaust pipes blaring—she trembled with hunger.

There was the time she was at the hotel bar in Riverside. There were two young college football players – one white and one black. The white one walked up to her at the bar and whispered in her ear. He said, "We want to eat your pussy," to which she had replied, "You better do more than that!" With a smile and a nod, she took his hand and led him back to her room. The black kid stood by the door. Things had only

just started when he began to shake. He started crying
and then stumbled off. This knocked the other kid so far
off his game that he quit, saying said it felt weird. He left
Ashley on her own as her breath started to leave her. She
finally got a half-hearted fuck from the maintenance man
she called to fix her shower-head at 2:00 AM.

Then there was the time she took a hike at the
park. At one of the secluded picnic areas she started
talking to a guy who seemed like a good candidate, and
just as soon as she had started rubbing his cock through
his cargo shorts, his wife showed up with a twin stroller
and an expression of barely-contained rage. He stumbled
off, calling after her.

There were guys who talked a good game and
couldn't deliver, and there were guys who could deliver
but needed to feel they were controlling the action—and
the latter couldn't stand to be approached by the woman
first. It threw them.

For the most part, men were just lousy lays,
treating her like a China doll or making her feel like they
were just masturbating inside of her. She had done men

as old as sixty-five and as young as eighteen (or so they told her). She had fucked them in cars, in the darkened corners of offices, at the park, and in a minivan in a church parking lot—one that she noticed had a "clergy" sticker on it as he led her up to it.

She belonged to several online swinger clubs. Her handle was "MsBonaparte" or always some variation on it. Not many men there recognized the allusion to Napoleon's sister – the one who had made a reputation for herself in taking on whole legions of her brother's army. To Ashley, Pauline Bonaparte had become an unlikely hero, or at least a partner in misery. At least she was much more of a hero than anyone she had met through the swinger clubs. There was something *off* about each of them–something missing from their energy. It was as though they had a hollow core, and most of them tried to make up a low quality of sexual skills with sheer numbers of contacts.

At some point after she realized that her one encounter with Raymond hadn't miraculously cured her, Ashley decided to try for a normal, healthy relationship with a man who could satisfy her needs, mainly just to

keep her alive. She still didn't feel a need to be in a
relationship for any other reason. There were multiple
problems in this endeavor. Mainly, she found that the
nice guys whom a young professional woman was
expected to date weren't able to do what she needed.
They didn't move with desire, but more with either a
self-conscious interest in their own pleasure or a sense of
obligation, or sometimes even despite a shame in what
they were doing. Most couldn't handle her when she
started expressing her herself and honestly demanding
what she needed. It scared them off.

*Harder, Scott! Do it harder! What is wrong with
you?*

*Take me, Brent. Goddamn it… what do you
fucking want? Do it! Just do it! Fuck me!*

*David, I want you to fuck me. Fuck me like a
little bitch.*

Fuck me like a whore. Just fuck me. Hard!

Troy…Troy… I've been fucked harder by

grandpas!

Ashley was usually disappointed in the efforts that followed. And after her angry exhortations, they usually had a talk. Thus the long (or short) march towards a break-up would start. But then, the ones who *could* move with desire often seemed dangerous or stupid. They had what she needed, but at what price?

Thus Ashley's attempts at ongoing relationships had failed, one after another. Things would start off great. As the man lost his initial interest or proved out as sexually lame in some way, she'd start feeling faint, and desperately seek attention from one of his friends or relatives or anyone else who could deliver. The humiliation was too much for a man, having put some sort of emotional investment into her, only to walk in and see her bouncing on his brother's cock. It was much safer for her to stay just at the sexual level to get what she needed and keep the emotions out of it—emotions she had really never felt in the first place.

*   *   *   *   *

As she drove along, her mind wandered over her surroundings. It was a hot afternoon in August. No one was on the street. She knew her body well enough to realize she might not make it out of the valley and into LA in time, and besides, she really didn't know anyone down there.

There was one place that she had seen in Indio that fascinated her in a dark way. She had driven by it hundreds of times over the years. She never had the nerve or inclination to actually go inside. But these were desperate times.

The Prius pulled into the dirt parking lot of the Irön Hög, which was little more than a grey shack off to the side of a frontage road. The dashboard said it was 115 degrees outside. She opened the door and felt the sweltering heat seeming to push her back inside. She felt her heart palpitate. There were only three or four Harleys and an old pickup parked outside, and the tiresome strains of *Freebird* floated out from the door and past the beer signs.

She walked inside. Two guys at a table hunched

over their beers. They looked up as the sunlight illuminated them and they squinted. Both wore gang colors on their vests. She could tell by looking at them that they were heroin addicts.

Forget that. She had memories of disgust and frustration all around that drug. In addition to almost ensuring one would get HIV, it made for lazy moves, limp dicks, and more desperation.

There was the distinct smell of dive bar in the air. It was a combination of stale beer, stale cigarettes, and stale piss.

Eyes from the shadows traced her as she walked to the bar. She felt a nervous weakness in her knees and hips, but did her best to keep herself together.

She took a seat at the bar. A blousy blonde in a red tank top sneered at her from the cash register. She approached, her eyes fixed on Ashley's neckline.

"Darlin', we don't want your kind in here right now, so ..." She nodded towards the door.

"What kind? A customer?"

"We don't want what you're sellin' here, you hear me?" She was getting a little angrier.

"I'm not selling anything. What are you accusing me of?"

"Now you see here, you *fu*..." Maude was reaching for a black billyclub beside the cash register.

Just then, Ashley felt a hand on her shoulder. The woman went quiet.

Ashley turned to see the pockmarked face of a guy in his mid-twenties. He looked at her nervously. He raised his lips in something approximating a smile, revealing rotten teeth. She looked into his eyes, or tried to, rather. It was apparent that he had suffered some sort of head injury at some time, and had been welded and glued back together in some sort of fleshy patchwork.

"You're real pretty," he said, his lips quivering.

Suddenly Ashley felt another pair of hands on her from the back. She turned her head just enough to see a fat, greasy face under a greasy mop of hair. This one was also sporting a mouthful of rotting teeth.

These were the fruits of meth: white-trash cocaine. And this was why she had avoided this place and others like it.

She felt the clammy hands grab her breasts from behind. She didn't want this. She tried pushing them away. The guy in front had decided to go for her between her legs, and his hands were creeping up her thighs. She glanced over her shoulder, scared. She saw the woman behind the bar smirk at her and turn away, going back to cleaning glasses. And just as Ashley turned back to face her tormentor, she felt the slobbering, stinking lips of the warped-looking man approaching. She drew her hand back and slapped him. He reeled back and snarled, then drew his fist back.

Then, as if descending from the heavens, a hand from behind him grabbed his fist. The guy with the broken face gasped and moaned as he was spun around to face his attacker. Ashley could see his crooked eyes bulging in pain.

"What did I tell you guys about the women?" She heard the voice before she saw its origin. The voice came through clenched teeth. "What did I tell you two *assholes* about the women?"

"I dunno… I …"

The guy behind Ashley with the clammy hands suddenly released her. She watched the warped man getting rammed towards the door, his head in something resembling a hammer-lock. His friend scampered beside him.

"You stay the fuck out of my establishment, you *pinche pendejo* motherfuckers. You go home and fuck your mothers, motherfucking pledge pieces of shit."

The door swung open as the warped man's face hit it, then closed, and they were gone.

He was a tall Hispanic—maybe about thirty-five—with a long moustache and beard tied together at its bottom with a sort of silver clasp. Some strands of grey had begun to appear in his long hair. He wore a vest with colors on it. A patch with an orange flaming skull said "CEBERUS MC" under it.

With the two losers thrown out, he straightened his vest and walked back towards Ashley. He visibly straightened his spine and checked his face in the mirror before he turned to her.

"I am really sorry there, uhh……Miss. Those guys ain't nothing but trouble."

"It's ok, really I just…"

"I really want to make it up to you. That's not the sort of thing we tolerate here at this establishment. I'm the owner here," he said, offering his hand. "They call me Chevo."

Ashley nervously straightened her hair and took his hand. His hands were large, calloused, yet gentle. His fingers were covered with turquoise and silver.

Maude glared at her, shifting her eyes to the Chevo from time to time.

"Hey Maude, she's OK. I want to buy this lady a beer. Get her a beer, Maude," he said in his softly accented English.

Maude sneered and went back to wiping down the counter.

Ashley looked into Chevo's eyes. She noticed he had a long scar that ran from beside his right eye down to the edge of his mouth.

"I'm Jennifer," Ashley lied. She was looking to fuck to stay alive, but there were still some risks she wouldn't take.

Chevo looked at her with a steely smile. His eyes were dark and deep-set. He nodded politely.

"Sure is hot out there. Nice to be inside, huh?" said Chevo. Ashley nodded and smiled. Maude put a mug of some sort of weasel-piss beer down in front of her, sneering and trying not to make eye contact.

"So what brings you in here today?" Chevo asked as he slowly lowered himself onto the stool beside her. Ashley allowed her eyes to wander to his jeans. Through the shadows, she thought she could see something making an impression.

"Just out for a drink. I saw this place and thought I'd try it out." Ashley shrugged, trying to seem nonchalant.

Two years before, just after confirming her diagnosis, she had thought that her condition would be easy to treat—all she would need to do was to walk up to the nearest man, lift her skirt, and say, "Fuck me." But she found out that usually scared them away. Even roughrider-looking badass-motherfuckers like Chevo. Most guys thought twice about sticking their dicks in a pretty little jar of crazy, no matter how nice and available it seemed to be.

Chevo's shoulders looked strong. Ashley took a sip of beer.

"So what really brings you here today? I mean… there are a lot of other places."

"I'm looking for, well…" She looked at him. She realized that if there were anyone in the building that day she could come close to trusting, it would need to be him.

He slowly allowed his hand to wander over to her wrist and then down to her knee, then her thigh. "Yes?" he asked as his fingers gently traced a line from her knee up to her hip.

"I need something," said Ashley. "And no, it's not drugs." There was a little quiver in her voice. She glanced at her watch. Whatever he was going to do, it would need to be within two hours or so.

"I understand," said Chevo. His hand rose up the outside of her arm and over her shoulder, tracing up her neck and cheek. His fingers arrived at her mouth. She was trembling. Gently, he pressed two fingers of his right hand to her mouth and he caressed her lips. She quivered. Her right hand jittered and moved towards his jeans. He felt so large, so hot.

She moved her head enough to get his fingers away from her mouth.

"Do you have a place… where we could go?" she asked haltingly.

Chevo's hand had been just close enough to touch the wetness on her inner thighs as he approached very close to her center. He smiled and slowly pulled his hand back.

"Yeah, I got a place," he said, a steely grin coming over his face.

He nodded to Maude as he got to his feet. He took Ashley's hand, and his head turned towards a door to the side of the bar. Ashley rose and grasped her purse. On the way there, Chevo looked at her and gestured with his finger up to tell her *one second*. Then he put several quarters into the jukebox. The strains of *Suavecito* came through the speakers.

Chevo was turning out to be a real gentleman. He even provided make-out music.

He returned to Ashley and escorted her back through the darkened corner to the office. The door shut behind them.

And then Chevo was on her. He took her and pressed her against the door, knocking her off-balance, but then catching her beneath her arms. His hand worked up and down her sides, down to her hips, squeezing her firmly but gently as his tongue worked its way into her mouth and she moaned. He grunted. She felt his hand working around to her front, squeezing and gently kneading her left breast. Ashley struggled to untie her dress before he could rip it off of her.

She felt the size and the hardness of his cock pressing hard against her mound. She tasted his tongue and it tasted like a spice. It was like cloves. It only made her want him more. The next thing she felt was his hand racing between her thighs. She was sopping wet, and when Chevo touched it, he chuckled a bit before gently delving first one, then two fingers into the soft wet folds of her hot, naked pussy.

Ashley was squeezing his dick through his pants and moaning.

"That what you want, *mamacita?* You want that?"

"Yes…"

"Then *tell me!*" Chevo growled as he pulled her hair. "Tell me what you fucking want."

"I…I want your fat cock in my wet…*cunt*. Fuck me …"

He took a fistful of her hair at the root and gently pulled. His fingers were lifting up on her pussy, pressing her against the door. She felt a wave of energy starting in her vagina and rising up the centerline of her body.

"First you need to get me started," he said. He pulled back and undid his belt. Ashley was leaning against the door, her whole world swirling. Chevo dropped his pants, and out sprang about eight inches of thick, dark, uncut, hard cock. His hair was untrimmed, but that did nothing to disguise the size of his package.

He was hard and pulsing, and his foreskin had pulled back, revealing a hot purple head. She leaned forward. Gently, he took her by her hair, and with the other hand, guided his cock to her lips. The swollen, tip pressed past her lips. Her tongue danced on the underside, rubbing the frenulum. She could taste the sweetness of his pre-cum.

"Mmmm…I like that tongue, *mamacita*. Here, you take me back in your throat. You just relax. You can do it."

With that he braced himself, took two fistfuls of her hair and firmly but gently started pushing back into her mouth. Ashley breathed out and tried to relax. He was straining against her. It was slow but unstoppable. It was running against some resistance. Chevo just pushed harder, slowly, almost imperceptibly. She felt something give way, and in a moment, Chevo's cock was in her throat. His hand was pressed against the back of her head. Her nose was buried in his musky pubes. And then he started fucking her throat.

"Oh fuck yeah, *mami.* That's what Chevo likes." He was gently, slowly, throat-fucking her. She felt his fat cock making a bulge in her throat. She wrapped her hands around his muscular ass and held it. In some way she felt life being pumped back into her. The hair on his dick felt raspy on her face, and she tasted him and inhaled his scent. There was slight sense of panic. But his cock in her throat wasn't what had her on edge. She was afraid he would cum too quickly, before she had a chance to take his glorious rod into her hungry, yearning pussy.

Then, he started pounding into her throat and she was gasping, trying to press against his thighs and to keep him from suffocating her. The thought of this bearded Mexican biker she had known for about five minutes fucking her throat in a dirty office while her dress draped over her shoulders made her burn. It started between her legs and went up to the top of her head.

She started to choke. She panicked, pounding her fists on his hips to get him to release her.

"You had enough, *mami*?" he released her. "You come up here."

Gently, he lifted her to her feet. She was panting. Her throat felt raw.

Sweetly, softly, he stroked her hair and then kissed her. His rough hands were now gentle on the skin of her breasts. He traced a line down her firm belly, over her hip, and to her wet, palpitating, naked mound.

"Yeah, that's what Chevo likes. I like to feel my cock in your mouth. Beautiful woman. Beautiful Jennifer. Come," he said. He gestured to the desk. With a rough sweep of his arm he cleared off half of it, sending papers, office supplies, an ashtray, and even a can of beer to the floor.

He took her by the arm and guided her to the desk, bending her down over it.

He reached behind her and roughly spread her ass cheeks apart, two fingers tracing a line from her clit, over her lips, and back to her anus. That was the one thing Ashely wouldn't do. She lifted up.

"No! Not there! Not in my ass!" she said.

"Relax, *mami.* Not gonna hurt you none. How about this…"

She felt his wet cock sliding around on the backs of her thighs. Its fat head rose up to her wet slit, and with one hand spreading her open, and the other guiding his tool, he slowly rubbed it all over her wet lips, taking his time to lubricate it. It was a wonderful and frustrating sensation all at once.

Then, carefully aligning his head with her entrance, he slowly drove his manhood into her.

It took her breath away.

"Yeah, that's what Chevo wants. You like that, *mami*?"

"*Yes …yes…*"

And he started pumping, slowly, at first. With every thrust, Ashley felt life being pumped back into her. And he got faster. Harder. He yanked back on her hips, grinding his pelvis up against hers. She felt a surge of excitement racing through her, up and down her spine, making her flex. She just wanted more and more. She felt his balls swinging up to touch her clit with every stroke.

"Take that cock. Take me in your cunt, you fucking slut!" he growled. "What are you? *What are you?*"

"I'm a dirty slut! Fuck my cunt!" Ashley growled as she looked over her shoulder at him.

"You're a whore. Dirty fucking *puta!*"

"Fuck me! Cum in me! I want your cum!" He was working up to a frantic and intense pace. He yanked her arms and pinned them behind her back, holding her wrists in place with one hand. With his other hand, he started slapping her ass. She felt his hard, calloused hand slamming against each cheek. The pain combined with the pleasure from his cock was intoxicating. He was alternating slaps with his strokes, which just got harder and harder. Her face was against the dirty surface of the desk. It was enough to make her pull up and try to move away, but she felt his forearm come down on her from behind.

"Don't move, slut. Daddy's fucking his little girl."

"Yes! Yes!" she gasped.

His strokes got even harder and more forceful. She felt the fronts of her thighs being driven into the edge of the desk. Then he seethed through his teeth as he went into an even faster and harder phase. Ashley suddenly felt a familiar sensation rising up out of her pussy. Suddenly wave after wave was flowing over her body. Her vaginal muscles fluttered and grasped at him. She shuddered and cried out with a breathy howl. And still he was pumping as hard as ever.

Slowly, he reduced his speed and intensity. She could hear him breathing through the ringing in her ears.

"You cum? You cum yet?"

She just gasped in a moaning voice that filled the room. She had found it. She found the guy who knew what to do. With that final burst of energy into her, she thought she could rejoin the land of the living. She would need to make other arrangements to meet up with him in a safer place going forward, whenever she needed it again. And she was almost hoping it wouldn't be too long before she felt the urge.

Then he said, "Well, now it's my turn."

He pulled out his dick, and she heard him spit. There was moisture on her ass as his finger pressed into it.

"*No*! *Not there*!" Ashley yelled.

"Come on, bitch. Round three."

She tried to pull away but he had her arms

pinned behind her. "No! *No!*" she was yelling. He slapped her ass again, harder than ever. She felt his finger probing her anus. The pain was searing already.

"C'mon. Don't fight it, slut. Take me in your ass. You know you want it, dirty ass slut." Chevo was flicking his cock over her asshole. He was so much taller and stronger than she. Her legs strained and flailed, but she couldn't move. She was still enervated from her orgasm, which felt like it was still going on. She felt him press the spongy head of his cock on her tightest hole.

Suddenly, the office door flew open. It was Maude.

"Chevo! Motherfucking narcs! It's a bust! Get your pants on!"

*   *   *   *   *

In the swirling panic that followed, Chevo yanked up his pants and ran out the back door, setting off an alarm.

The room was filled with the a shrieking siren. Ashley had just lifted herself up off the tabletop when the SWAT team rammed though the doorway past Maude, assault rifles in hand and ski masks covering their faces. Maude tumbled to the floor with a scream as the cops shouted into their radios. Ashley hit the desk, feeling exposed.

In the background, she heard a Harley starting up and revving away in the distance, then sirens as the cops tumbled out the door, swearing orders into their radios.

Ashley slowly lifted herself up off the desk. She wrapped and tied the dress around her middle, and tried to re-arrange her hair without benefit of a mirror. She picked her purse up off the mess on the floor. She took a tissue and wiped the last of her lipstick off, and casually popped an Altoid. Maude had run back out into the restaurant and was swearing at the cops at the top of her lungs. Ashley looked around. Showing nerve she had perfected over two years of being forced to get what she needed to live through the most unlikely and dangerous means, she quickly gathered her senses and walked out through the back door.

As she emerged, she saw three SUVs with lights and sirens chasing Chevo as he rode away down the highway, loud pipes blaring on his chopper. Ashley's Prius was still parked in front. One patrol car was still parked in the lot, and she heard crashes, swearing, and protests coming from inside the building.

She straightened her back, put on her sunglasses, and walked out to her car. In two minutes, she was rolling back down the highway towards Palm Springs.

The last waves of her orgasm still rippled through her body, up from her pleasantly-sore vagina, over her clitoris, through her abdomen. Her nipples felt almost too sensitive as the wind from the air conditioner vent blew the smooth polyester surface of her dress against her. The slight tinge of pain from Chevo's finger in her butt barely distracted her. Despite the discomfort and the fear and the disgust she felt at having almost been anally raped, she had to admit that he knew what he was doing. He had been an expert at rough-fucking. He had moved with desire. And she hoped in the back of her mind that he would somehow give the cops the slip and not end up scattered across I-10 somewhere, or riddled with bullets after carjacking someone he just might end up killing—if he had to.

He had been a solid and exciting fuck, and she longed for the feeling of his cock again in her still-wet pussy. He was welcome, as long as he stayed away from her ass. And she wondered if he ever could.

If he had come inside of her, it would probably have been enough to get her through her crisis. It was that intense and that good. But through the internal post-coital fog in her body, she could tell that it wouldn't be long before the symptoms rose up. Inside of her was a voice chanting "More! More! More!"

She looked at the clock. She felt her heart skip. It was now a little after two. If she couldn't get rid of these flutters in an hour or so, she'd need to be close to a hospital and hope for the best.

It was now 118 degrees outside. As she entered the flow of traffic on I-10, she wondered where to go next. It seemed that the pavement itself was melting.

In times of crisis, it's common to go to the places one knows best. People tend towards the familiar. Though she hated the thought that it might only mean she would collapse in public and be taken to a hospital and drugged up – only to feel her life fall away from her – downtown Palm Springs called out to her.

She exited I-10 at Palm Canyon and drove south, passing mansions, golf course, resorts, and shops that catered to the ultra-wealthy. As she approached Alejo Drive, her eyes went to the parking lot of the building of HammerCo Investments. They were closed on Sundays, and the parking lot was empty.

Or rather, it was empty but for the presence in the first space right outside the door of a gray Bentley Continental. It was Mr. John Hammer's personal car.

Wild thoughts entered Ashley's mind.

She had seen Mr. Hammer in the office many times, though had never been introduced. He usually had a bodyguard or two around him. He was always whisked in and out of the building in a discreet way. It was said he was one of the wealthiest men in California—if not the world. Thus, it was important to keep certain specifics about him a secret. Even most photos of him had been edited or altered in some way to keep his identity a mystery.

Ashley looked at the car and surmised that it might have been driven there by one of Mr. Hammer's bodyguards, who had seemed totally uninterested in her when she would occasionally greet them in an elevator. Mr. Hammer had very strict rules about fraternizing on the job.

Ashley had tried so very hard over the last two years to keep her medical issue separate from work. In her business as an auditor, fucking someone at work could mean career suicide. She had been successful in keeping her hands to herself in the workplace, and everyone else's off her.

While waiting at the light, she glanced across the street at a café. An old couple dressed in matching white tennis outfits had just parked their Mercedes and were helping their Pomeranians out of the backseat. A couple of skinny guys in shorts and sunglasses sat under the misters, looking gayer than gay. There were no prospects there.

Ashley looked back at the Bentley in the parking lot. She reached into her glove box and pulled out her ID badge, the one that would get her into the building.

With a beep and a whoosh, the door opened into the vacant lobby. It was almost chilly inside. The lights were down throughout the building. She could hear her own breath. She made a short detour to the ladies room to clean up and re-apply her lipstick and mascara.

As she took the elevator up to the third floor where Mr. Hammer's office occupied one corner of the building, she felt her breath suddenly get irregular. She tried thinking of other places around the neighborhood that could serve if this fell through—someplace where the median age was less than sixty-five and not everyone was a gay male. She hoped that she would still be strong enough to drive when she needed to leave, if nothing happened.

The elevator door opened with a soft *ding*. The large office floor covered with gray cubicles was cool and half-lit from sunlight coming through the blinds. At the opposite end of the room, was Mr. Hammer's office. The door was slightly ajar.

As she approached, Ashley heard a voice inside. It was soft, determined, and bore a certain angry energy. It sounded desperate in a way. She couldn't make out what he was saying. It sounded as if it were something about the end or an end. It repeated again and again.

She stood back from the door, not knowing if she dared open it. The voice continued.

"All that for this…all that for this…this is how it ends," it chanted, breathily. It was the sound of absolute devastation.

Ashley straightened her back and knocked on the door. There was a sudden gasp.

"Who is it? Open the door!" the voice demanded. Ashley tipped the door open. As it moved further, she saw a man sitting behind an enormous desk. And though she had only seen him from a distance while being shuffled from one appointment or another, she recognized him as Mr. Hammer.

In his hand was a Glock pistol. He held it close to his chest, not pointing it in any particular direction.

"Yes?" he asked, the deep frown on his face lifting a bit as his eyes traveled over her body.

"Yes?" he asked again.

"I…" Ashley was dumbstruck "I saw your car and thought …"

"And thought what?" He scowled, though his expression was softening. He set the pistol on the desk and pushed it away.

"I wanted to make sure …" her voice trailed off.

"Make sure? Make sure of what? Do you work here, Miss?" he demanded. But then with a second thought, he winced and made a motion with his head as though suddenly realizing that he had been forgetting himself.

"I'm sorry, I see your badge. How can I help you? I'm John Hammer." He still seemed deeply troubled, but was putting on a brave face and trying to pull himself together, making an effort at the self-confident social front that suited a successful, ultra-wealthy capitalist.

"And you are?" he asked.

"Ashley, Ashley Roarke. I'm in audit."

"Ah yes, audit… audit," he said gravely as his jaw tightened.

Ashley looked at the Glock on the desk. There was also a laptop computer opened next to him. Off to his side was a stack of papers on top of a manila envelope.

He was a tall man with a chiseled jaw, and wore his forty-two years with an almost divine masculine grace. His face showed about three days of beard growth. He wore a green pastel polo shirt that covered his toned pectorals, and his full head of salt and pepper hair made him look distinguished, with just the right patina of maturity. He looked like a sad Greek god, angered over the loss of a love thought to have been immortal. He drummed his fingers on his desk nervously and looked at the Glock as though he had been interrupted.

"Mr. Hammer?" asked Ashley. "I found myself without anything to do this afternoon and I, well, decided to come in and maybe—you know—reorganize some files. But I wonder …" she paused and glanced at the gun.

"Ashley, come in and have a seat," said Mr. Hammer. He pointed at the expensive Danish office chair on the opposite side of the desk. Ashley tried to regain her ladylike composure as she sat down, if only out of habit.

"Ashley, how long have you been with us?"

"Five years, Mr. Hammer."

"John. Call me John." He still wasn't smiling. He slowly got up from his desk and walked to a cadenza on the opposite wall, introspectively gazing into the mirror above it. He touched a button, and with a whirring sound the mirrored panel lowered, revealing a fully stocked bar.

"Five years, eh? That's quite a while. Would you care for a..." he trailed off while pouring himself a scotch into a highball glass. Ashley shook her head as she looked at his strong ass under his expensive Italian slacks. There was still a tension about him as he walked back to his desk chair. He took a swig.

"Five years ago, I never would have thought I'd be here, Ashley. Back then, I felt successful. I felt I was helping others in their careers. I felt I had the right relationship. But let me tell you: all of that can change in an instant." He chuckled, ruefully. "It's remarkable how quickly that can change. You see, you need to sacrifice a lot to get to the top. You really do. And sometimes when you make it, it's not all it seems. You start to think about whether or not it's worth it."

"Mr. Hammer, I mean John—I don't think anyone would say they don't appreciate you and what you've done for them. I mean, I've been happy here. I've been …"

"You've been used, Ashley. You've been used." His voice rose for a moment, a ruefullness almost overtaking it. "And I have used you and others, and now I've been used." His voice faded away to a murmur. He brought his hand to his mouth. He looked stricken.

"I don't understand." Ashley shook her head.

John Hammer leaned forward from his slouch in his chair, reached across his desk, and slowly pushed the documents stacked on top of a manila envelope across the smooth walnut desktop towards Ashley.

"DIVORCE FILING," it stated at the top. Claimant was Martje R. De Vries-Hammer of 126

Palmcrest Drive, Palm Springs. Respondent was John R
Hammer.

"Oh John, I am so very sorry to hear about this,"
said Ashley, wondering if he had been drinking very
long and whether the gun was really loaded. And of
course, her heart leapt with excitement as much as it
could in her state.

"But you can recover! It happens all the time,
I'm sorry to say." She looked at him expectantly. "By
the way John, do you need ..."

John laughed cynically. "All the time! All the
time, she says. All the time!" John leaned forward and
turned the laptop towards Ashley. On the screen was a
graph showing total accounts. She was familiar with the
report from her work in audit. On previous Friday, only
two days before, the graphs showed the accounts had
suddenly dropped by something approaching 98%.
Hundreds of billions in value had been wiped out in a
single day. It was almost too much for her to process.

She flipped through the divorce filing and got to

another set of documents behind the first, printed on different paper. It was a grand jury summons for indictments on money laundering and wire fraud. The defendant was John R. Hammer.

Ashley's jaw dropped. This just didn't make sense.

"She's in Switzerland now, along with whatever was left of the firm's money. Took off with her Reiki therapist. I caught them by the pool on Wednesday. Guess she had this planned for a while. Ratted me out to the FBI from the airport before she took off in my Gulfstream."

"Oh, Mr. Hammer...I...I don't know what to say. "

"There's nothing to say." He shook his head as he looked down at his drink. "We're out of business. Come tomorrow, the customers and associates I've known for years will be here, asking what happened." He looked at his iPhone. "Some are already trying to get a hold of me." He shook his head again.

"I went to so many of their kid's weddings and birthday parties. Introduced a lot of them to their spouses. That's all gone now. I see where it all led." He breathed a heavy sigh and glanced at the gun.

He set the glass down on the desk and tapped his fingernails on the surface anxiously.

"Ashley, it's been nice working with you. And I'm glad you could come in to say…well…hello, I guess. I really wish I could help you, but I'm afraid I'm a bit limited right now." On his face was an expression of absolute despair.

"I think you'd best be going now. And thank you for all you've done." He nodded gravely.

Ashley's eyes went down to the pistol again.

"Mr. Hammer—John—please…are you? I mean."

"You'll probably want to leave. I want you to leave. Go."

Ashley leapt to her feet. "*No! I will not leave!*" she almost snarled. As she stood up, she felt the blood drain from her head. She felt dizzy and faint. She glanced at the clock on the wall. The time was getting close, and *this* had to happen?

"You need help. You can't do this!" she pleaded.

"There's nothing else to do. I was a fool. I couldn't be trusted. I couldn't even trust ..."

Ashley walked around to behind his desk, keeping one hand on it while she walked.

"John, you have so much to live for," she said, touching his shoulder.

"I have nothing to live for. No. I don't. I have nothing."

"John, John, listen to me. I need you."

"No one needs me. I am a fool."

"John...please, won't you listen?" Ashley looked at him. His face was starting to form a pout. She thought she could see a tear welling up in his eye. "John ..."

Ashley looked at this beautiful man in the prime of his life, slowly letting himself be reduced to a blubbering mess, and inside of her rose up a festering bloom of righteous anger. In one moment of impulse, she stood up straight, sneered, pulled her right hand back far beside her, then slapped him hard across his face.

His drink fell to the carpet. His hand came up to his cheek. His eyes opened wide. He gasped.

Ashley leaned towards him. She spoke softly, but with a deep intensity that only grew.

"John...John...I'm going to tell you one thing right now that is very, very important and very, very real. I need you. And I need you right now. And I know you lost your wife and your jet and your billions, but let me tell you, none of that ever meant anything. Because at least you *have* a life! You have a life that isn't being taken from you. And here you are trying to take it from yourself…over a stupid…fucking…*airplane?*"

At that, Ashley staggered backwards. Her head was getting lighter. She looked at the expensive clock on the wall just over John's head. It was getting blurry. She reached down to untie the wrap-around dress, but her fingers weren't listening to her.

John looked at her, his eyes covering every inch of her body. She felt her breath getting shallow.

"Ashley, I …" he looked at her as though he were trying to come to terms with what was laid out before him. "I didn't expect …"

He held his cheek and gazed at her. He straightened his back in his chair. There was a sudden hardness that came over his expression. Color was coming back into his cheeks. Ashley sensed the change. She thought she was onto something.

"Ashley, I don't think you understand what I'm up against here, and what's been going on with…"

She staggered towards his chair. She raised her hand and slapped him again. A surge of rage came over his expression.

"Is it going to be like that, you …you …?" she taunted him. She was losing focus. She could barely feel her fingers.

"Ashley …" His tone was deeper, suddenly more serious.

"I know what you want. You pansy. I have it, but you're not man enough to take it." Ashley was hoping that she was right this time. John's eyes narrowed. His teeth clenched.

"*You're a …*" he growled.

"A what? Say it. Can you tell me what I am, Johnny? Little Johnny?" Her voice took on a sweet, teasing condescension. "Because I can tell you what you are. Your wife knew and I know. You're a crying little…"

John leapt to his feet. "*You shut up, you fucking
…*" He seethed as he grabbed Ashley by the throat with
one hand, the other roughly clutching her arm. Ashley
snatched the arm that held her throat. The adrenaline was
waking her up.

"You couldn't keep your wife," said Ashley,
gasping for air through his grip. "She fucked her Reiki
teacher. How does that feel, John? You probably tasted
his cock on her lips. How was that, John?" she shouted
in a screeching, gravelling voice that was taking
everything out of her.

"I loved her…I …" He shouted. His brow
furrowed. He was starting to come apart.

"You loved money. That's all."

"No! You…*you* …"

"You are a coward. Does your dick even …" At
that, John drew his hand back to slap Ashley, but then he
looked down at her hard nipples poking through the
fabric of her dress. His arms were tense, but he released

her. Ashley staggered back and looked down and saw something prodding from the front of his expensive grey Italian slacks.

He charged at her, a rage storming over his complexion. Grabbing her dress with both hands, he ripped it from her, revealing her pert nipples and full breasts. He picked her up under her arms, lifting her onto the desk in front of him, sending the laptop and the papers to the floor. He leaned in and kissed her, clumsy with overpowering passion. Dazed, she reached down and pulled at his shirt. He grasped and pulled it over his head, revealing his strong, toned chest. She put his hands on her breasts then guided one down to her hot slit. He was getting the idea. He still seemed confused. He was clumsy. She reached for his belt. His pants dropped. And his semi-hard erection poked out of his boxers. He was decently sized but barely hard at all.

He looked at her and squeezed his dick, stroking it half-heartedly. "I usually have my pills before." He suddenly looked frustrated and ashamed. She was afraid he was going to cry again.

Ashley felt her heart starting to flutter. This could *not* be happening. She tried not to think of what had just been revealed to her over the last few minutes. She would need a new job. As an auditor she'd probably be implicated in the grand jury investigation. But for those things to matter, she would need to survive the next fifteen minutes.

Then, she remembered something.

She groped behind her, feeling around for where last she remembered seeing the one thing that could probably help her. It was her last chance. She felt a little to the right of her. Table. Table. Table. Ahhh...there it was.

Her right hand slowly lifted the nine-millimeter Glock and pointed it at John Hammer. Remembering something from her concealed weapons class, she slid the action back, chambering a round.

"John, you're going to fuck me," she paused, winded from lifting the gun. "Or I'm going to kill you."

His eyes widened, and she looked down and beheld his cock. In seconds, it had grown to a very hard seven inches or so. Its head was a raging purple. He moved towards her and rubbed the head of his dick on her slit. She felt his desire course through him. He slid into her just as her vision was fading, and as he pounded into her, gradually increasing his rhythm and intensity, he shouted at her through it all. He shouted about his wife. He shouted about his wasted years.

Then he shouted about the Sinaloa cartels and the DEA and the Saudis and the Israelis and people in Rome and Washington and the CIA. All of the money was dirty. All of it was going to secret projects, most of them criminal. The government had known all along, and had set him up as a patsy from the beginning. With every revelation he fucked her even harder, curling his spine up to drive it into her while touching parts inside that had never been reached before. All of his rage and fear and frustration poured out of him and into her, and the rage itself was like a wave of energy that sustained her.

Then finally, with the blackness vented from

him, desire came.

When she first lifted the gun she was barely conscious. As he fucked her, she gradually felt her sensation return to her fingers. Breath filled her lungs again. And she looked up and John suddenly came into focus—all of him. His sweating, raging, excited, vulnerable and insanely energetic self.

He paused for a moment, then took her hand and took the gun from her. He set it down on the table beside them. He turned his attention back to her. He looked into her eyes, deeply. There was something between them—two disordered souls thought to be lost, finally finding each other. He smiled. Then, he started again slowly, but his intensity grew. Suddenly there was a great surge of power from his muscular hips, and with a great roar he came, shouting and screaming "*Fuck! Fuck! Fuck!*". He erupted just as her own orgasm peaked and her muscles fluttered.

And suddenly Ashley's breath returned in a surge of elation and she could see clearly again. Her whole body trembled as life coursed back into her.

John collapsed on the desk next to her: both of them naked, both vulnerable, both needing each other to survive.

After a few seconds of panting, Ashley gathered her senses. "Thanks, I needed that," she said with a smile.

"Me too," said John, mustering a slight smile from the corner of his mouth.

"I know," said Ashley. And in some moment of what she would later recognize as clumsy-but-heartfelt, he lifted his arm and welcomed her against his muscled and sweating chest. Slowly, and tenderly, Ashley leaned against him, and looking up at him, they kissed.

*   *   *   *   *

Thirty minutes later, Ashley and John were in his Bentley with the air conditioner blasting. He had given her an oversized company t-shirt and one of his golf jackets to cover her in place of her ripped dress. They sat in the car as Ashley looked through the indictment and the divorce filing.

"I think you should just be happy you didn't have kids with this woman," she said disbelievingly. "She really...geez ..."

"Yes, she fucked me over."

"And the indictment ..." Ashley just shook her head as she looked it over. She sensed John tensing up. She looked at him. "John, we can find someone to help. With all you know, with all the dirt you have on so many, you have leverage."

"I have enough leverage to get myself killed. And now, you're involved. So they'll probably take an interest in you as well. I am so sorry, Ashley."

"I still think there's a way. You have enough information on your laptop to hang so many of them."

"If they don't kill me first," he said, gritting his

teeth.

"They were counting on you to kill yourself, John."

His shoulders slumped. Slowly, a smile came to the corner of his mouth. Tenderly, he reached across and placed his hand on Ashley's. He looked her in the eye.

John Hammer looked out the windshield through the parking lot, searing in the summer heat. He looked up at the building he had built on a solid reputation, carefully manicured, all based on an utter lie. He looked back at Ashley.

"How far are we from the Mexican border?" he asked.

5

How Far to Go With It, and What To Do Next

He flexed inside of her and yanked her hips back towards him as he growled and grunted.

Yeah...pussy...tight fuckin' pussy...yeah.

She moaned and shuddered and felt his sweat on her back. They were both spent. This was just their victory lap.

The phone beeped.

Neither she nor her lover was tempted to reach across to the nightstand. To do so at that moment would have risked knocking her holstered pistol, her ID badge, and the phone itself to the carpet, possibly followed by the uncapped bottle of mineral water and whatever was left in the highball glass. Duty called, but at least it had shown the common decency to wait a bit this time around.

The evening had started off as it usually did for their get-togethers. She showered, shaved, and put on a pair of older, pilled-up cotton panties and a shapeless bra. She rolled on a pair of black thigh-highs with false seams in the back. Then she got into one of the rather plain and unfashionable old dresses she bought at thrift stores specifically for these occasions.

She checked the mirror. She needed a little lipstick touch-up. She had already decided her medium-length, wavy, ash-blonde locks were ready for a new look. She made a mental note to set a hair appointment as she primped. It would be easier in the week that followed, which promised to be less busy than the last. She hoped she wouldn't need to go to the office. Her hair would be a mess in the morning.

Five minutes before the appointed time, she sat in her living room and pretended to scan over the latest reports she had brought home, only partially self-conscious about the clunky red flamenco shoes she was wearing. He liked the way those shoes looked on her, though they didn't go with this outfit at all.

On her flat-screen TV, a *Seinfeld* rerun was playing with the sound turned down. She had seen it a few times before. Even though she knew what was to come during the show, tension still hung in the air as she watched it out of the corner of her eye. She saw Kramer burst into Jerry's apartment like she knew he would, and there was still some sense of shock and wonder in it, even though she had seen this same episode at least five times since she was at Yale back in the '90s.

Then came a knock on her door: three taps, then one, then one more. Acting the part of the foolish little girl, she rushed to the door, her senses on high. She turned the knob and pulled.

The door swept open with a rush and pushed her backwards. She gasped and jumped out of the way. He burst into the house–tall, athletic, wearing jeans, a brown leather jacket and a ski mask. He slammed the door behind him and locked it. Trembling, she turned, screamed and ran, but not fast enough.

He caught her by her wrist near the dining room table, then slammed her backwards against the wall with a thump.

"No, no!" she pleaded as he grabbed her by the root of her ash blonde curls. He swore and snarled as he leered down at her and thrust his crotch against her. His muscular body towered over her short, voluptuous frame.

Then his strong hands methodically grasped the modest neckline of the dress and ripped it from her, destroying the seams. With his strong hands on her shoulders, he pushed her to the floor.

She was dazed. "Anything! Anything! Just don't hurt me! I'll do anything!" she pleaded as she gazed up at him. The ceiling light shone around his head, still covered in a black ski mask. She could almost see him smiling through it.

"Yes, you will," he said.

A collapsible metal baton appeared from the

inside pocket of his jacket. With a sharp flick of his wrist, it snapped to full length, making a chilling metallic *thunk* as it extended. A surge came over her. She trembled with excitement.

This is new. This is good.

He reached down, took a handful of her hair, and slowly pulled her to her feet. Facing her towards the dining room, he grabbed the back of her neck.

Yes!

In a single motion, she was bent over her long dining-room table. He set the baton down next to her.

He yanked and gathered her wrists behind her, held them together with his right hand, and used the left to pull a wide zip-tie from his jacket. With expert dexterity, he wrapped it around her wrists and yanked it closed. It hurt, but just enough. He had been trained very well, she thought.

He moved his hands inside the remnants of her

ripped dress and found the seam at the side of her dingy white underwear. He roughly seized them at their weakest point and ripped. She gasped and involuntarily flexed her hips. She felt vulnerable and very alive– finally. She trembled just knowing how much she got off on the feeling of being savagely taken. Just thinking about *how* it excited her enflamed her senses.

The ripped panties dangled from her right hip. He forced her face-down against the table with his elbow and roughly spread her cheeks. With two thick, hot fingers, he gently stroked her lips. They were already slick with moisture. She quivered.

"Shaved, huh?"

"Yes…yes…" she said, her voice full of nervous anticipation.

"Where I come from, only sluts shave their pussies. Are you a slut?"

"Don't hurt me! I'll do anything!"

"I asked you if you were a slut."

She turned her head and looked at him over her shoulder. Her eyes narrowed. "I'm...I'm a *slut*." There was a raw, guttural growl in the last word.

He doffed his jacket and quickly unfastened his black leather belt. He yanked it out from his pants. She heard it snap as it pulled free from the last loop.

"Sluts get whipped," he said flatly.

"NO! No! Please!"

"Take it, slut."

The first blow landed on her curvy bottom with a *thwack*. The pain raced through her body with an exquisite tingle. Glowing warmth emanated from her backside, and she tried to stifle her screams lest the neighbors hear. She tried to lift up from the table, but he forced her back down.

"I said sluts get whipped! You chose to be a

whore. *Take the pain, whore!*"

The blows came harder, again and again. She grovelled under the intensity. Every cell in her body felt alive. The pain surged through her with every *thwack*, and she wept with joy and release. He knew exactly how far to go with it, and what to do next.

He stopped. She was shivering and gasping, her mouth quivering. He separated her lips, and with care he inserted two fingers into her hot, wet tunnel. She felt her toes curl and her hips flex to meet his suddenly tender touch of pleasure. The two fingers worked into her, massaging her and gently playing with her innermost bumps and curves. His other hand gently soothed the hot, reddened flesh of each cheek. Her entire pussy and the insides of both thighs were drenched in moisture. Then, with three fingers of his other hand gathered together, he gently drew scintillating circles around her tightest hole. She shuddered and moaned.

"Get up here." He grabbed her hair again and pulled her upright.

"Let's see those tits."

He pulled out a switchblade from his pants pocket, and with a quick slice of her bra, her pendulous breasts spilled out. He seized them and pulled on her hard nipples.

"Suck your tits, bitch." He shoved her right breast to her mouth and pulled her head down. Her mouth met her large, brown nipple. "Yeah, that's what I like to see. Do it. Do the other one."

"You like that, huh slut?"

"No!" Her refusal came as a yelp. Her eyes darted at him. She was defiant, but at the same time she looked forward to whatever punishment he was going to mete out for her impertinence.

"What do you mean 'no'? You're a fucking whore. You'll like what I want you to like."

"I don't like it!" She was trying to shake her head, though he held her firmly by her hair. Her voice was trembling.

"Then what do you like?" his hand was suddenly around her neck. "What do you want, whore?"

"I…I don't want *anything* from you!"

"You're going to suck my cock, whore. I'm going to sit in this chair, and you're going to beg to suck my cock."

He dropped his pants and stepped out of them, revealing his hard, thickly-veined member. It was already gleaming and slick.

"Now, how do you ask, nicely?"

"I…don't…" He grabbed the baton off the table.

"Please, please, may I suck your cock?"

"Suck my cock? That what you want, slut? And who am I?"

"Sir. Please may I suck your cock, sir?"

"Yes, you may."

She got to her knees slowly and carefully. Having her arms bound made it difficult and especially humiliating. The hardwood floor pained her knees. But it wouldn't be even that simple. She leaned forward to take his cock in her mouth, and just as she was about to make contact, he withdrew.

With his legs, he slowly pushed the chair back and away from her. The dining room chair slid along the hardwood floor, keeping his cock just out of reach from her lips.

She crept across the floor towards him on her knees. Almost despite herself, she yearned to have the taste of his cock on her tongue, to feel his fullness in her mouth. He kept slowly backing up, tantalizing her, watching her through his mask as she crawled and whimpered. Just when she'd get close and lower her mouth to him, he'd move again.

Halfway across the floor toward the opposite wall, she lost her balance, wobbled and fell. He broke out in deep, masculine laughter. He laughed at her as she struggled to get back to her knees with her hands tied behind her back. She fumed. He had already taken so much of her pride; he might as well take it all. She wanted the last shred of dignity ripped from her. She longed to be laid out naked, scrutinized, probed.

He stared at her and laughed while he stroked his dick. She heard his deep laughter. Looking up, she could see him stroking his dick. She could tell he was almost ready to end this part of the game.

As a testament to her fitness and her willpower, she finally got to her knees again and continued her harrowing journey of debasement.

"Please, Sir... please..." Somewhere in her were tears that wanted to fall, but didn't.

Finally the back of his chair touched the wall, and she caught up to him.

She had to use her body and neck to move. Her tongue danced into the wide hole at the tip and behind the crown. Hungrily she lapped him. Up and down the shaft she went with her tongue and lips, down to his balls, which had gathered into a tight package. She tried sucking at them. She was frustrated that he would do nothing to help her besides moving his cock slightly out of her way.

She noticed his familiar scent. It was pungent and seemed to be getting more so. It just made her want him more. She longed to be able to guide his rod into her mouth with her hands, pleasuring him while she squeezed and stroked. He was shaved bare as well, which she surmised made him a "slut" just like her – though she didn't dare mention it. It would have been difficult anyway, considering how her mouth was filled with his thickness as she bobbed her head up and down. Finally, he pressed the back of her head to gag her with his cock.

She heard him groan as his thighs shuddered. He was responding to her touch. She looked up at him and could see his eyes through the holes in the ski mask.

This was working for both of them.

"On your feet, slut. You've proven you're a bitch who will do anything for cock." He was almost winded.

She struggled to her feet. The remnants of her clothing hung on her. He leaned back on the chair. She stood before him. He reached to the table and grasped the collapsible baton. In the coldest, most deliciously inhuman way he could, he traced the curves of her hips and her pendulous breasts with the cold metal.

"Spread your legs" he commanded.

The baton traced its way over her abdomen and down to the wetness between her legs. The cold metal lingered on her mound as she shuddered. His other hand slowly worked his hard cock, alternately with the strokes he made as he prodded her with the baton. He got even harder as he turned to whacking the underside of her left tit with the baton, making her wince with each contact.

How evil, how delightfully devious it would be

for him to masturbate himself to completion in front of her–leaving her in a state of painful arousal, moisture from her pussy gliding down both of her thighs. He could finish and leave her there with her hands behind her back and no means of finishing herself. That would be almost too cruel even for him, but the night had already provided some unexpected pleasures and pains.

Suddenly, he stood up. Again, he took her by her hair in one hand and turned her around. She felt the cold metal of the baton sliding against her rear entrance from behind and slowly, firmly sliding forward to touch her slit. He applied upward pressure and turned her to the side with the baton as though it were a lever. He pulled the remnants of the bra off of her arms, then in a quick motion, wrapped it around her neck. He yanked it against her throat, pulling her upwards.

"Bedtime, slut. Time to try out those other holes," he sneered.

The pressure from the baton against her pussy lifted her up. With the bra pulling at her neck and her arms still tied behind her, he guided her towards the

D.M. Cobray

bedroom on tippy-toes. She could barely breathe. When they entered the bedroom, he pushed her from behind, dashing her face-down on the bed, her feet still on the floor. She felt dizzy with anticipation. In a single motion, he slid his cock into her from behind. It surged past her lips, no faster than was pleasurable, no slower than necessary. She sighed and gasped. Once inside of her, he retracted almost to the point that his head had pulled free, then furiously slammed against her. She was thrilled at the feeling of his long, sensuous strokes within her.

He snarled and growled savagely. *"I'm going to rape your cunt until you bleed!"*

"Yes, yes! Hard! Harder!" Something inside of her growled as sounds emerged.

She moaned at the intense sensation of his hand on her already sensitive ass. He slapped her ass and grunted, alternately pulling her bound wrists and yanking her hips up to meet his strokes. She felt wave after wave of pleasure mixed with pain with every movement.

He stopped, then lifted her up by her hips and moved her towards the middle of the bed. He applied pressure with both of his hands, forcing her to arch her back. Her rear felt very exposed. She missed having him inside of her. His fingers lingered on her ass, teasing her tight hole. Her heart was racing.

Then he grasped her hips and positioned himself behind her, teasing her slit with the large head of his cock, sliding it fast up and down from her clit up to her ass and back down again. *Smack!* He slapped the redness of her bottom again, sending a searing jolt of delicious pain through her. He slid his cock against her clit and just rubbed it for a few seconds as his thumb enticingly circled her rear entrance, teasing both of her most sensitive spots in a way that she found both exciting and frustrating. Finally, he settled his head against her wet lips and slid his cock back into her pussy with a single motion. She gasped.

He moved his feet to either side of her. He was almost a foot taller than she, which was how she liked it. She wanted to be his fuck doll. With her face on the bed and her ass up and her back arched, he again pressed his large cock even deeper into her throbbing sex. She moaned.

He started to thrust in and out, varying deep and shallow strokes. He pulled on her hips as he towered above her. The sensations were overwhelming her. The rhythm was intoxicating.

She felt the warmth building within her. Her muscles began to tense up around his cock, seeming to grasp at his every withdrawal. She enjoyed hearing his moans and growls as he hammered his cock into her, getting faster and more intense with each passing second. Her bones felt like they were rattling against his.

And then she felt his hand grasping her hair yet again as he moved to his knees behind her. He pulled up and back, hard, jerking her upright. Pain and excitement shot through her as she hung, helpless as a rag doll. She moaned and gasped. A white-hot wave of pleasure started in her core and shot out to every part of her body. It began as a tightening, and then became an undulating wave of pure sensation that washed over her. She gasped and writhed. She heard a strange, breathy, howling voice in the distance, only to realize it was her own. His seed filled her.

A smile came to her lips as she pondered him. Yet again, he had proven a master of the game.

A few seconds later, the phone went off.

"Yeah...pussy...tight fuckin' pussy...yeah."

Then came the second thoughts. *We really aren't supposed to be doing this.* Not now, when she was on call–like she always was.

She groaned and sighed as he slowly let her down on the rumpled white surface of the fine duvet. She heard the switchblade again, and with a flick, her arms were released. They ached. Gently, she flexed and relaxed her arms as she moved them around. Her scalp ached. Her rear ached. But as the air filled her lungs again, there was a beautiful feeling of peace.

She surmised that it had been a good experience for him as well. Unlike so many other times, there had

D.M. Cobray

been no inconveniently-timed *beep-beep-beep* to break their concentration.

A gentle golden aura seemed to surround her. Then came the *beep-beep-beep* again. She reached for the company phone, fumbling past the other objects on the nightstand. He fell on the bed beside her, still breathing heavily.

"Fucking phone!" he said. He yanked the ski mask off. Sweat covered him. He reached for one of her pillows and used it to wipe his face. It was hot in Washington D.C. that August night.

"It's ok, hey…" she said softly. "That was good. All good."

She took the secured, encrypted Android phone. She held it up to her face, and a focussed blue light flashed as it scanned her retina.

Then the screensaver flashed off and the message appeared in bold, capital letters:

SECTOR 7: DELIUS– DECISION PROTOCOL STAT:::

Her eyes widened. This couldn't be right.

"What's up?" he said, pulling two Davidoff cigarettes from the pack and setting the solid platinum ashtray on the bed between them.

"Can I take care of that for you?" he asked, just before inserting two cigarettes in his mouth and striking the lighter.

"Trace," she said softly, still staring at the messages that scrolled up the screen. "No Trace, you can't get this one. I'm afraid."

"What? Well, I mean, Jeanette…" he stopped himself. Even though he had been as intimate with her as a man could be only moments before, he knew there were things she couldn't share. She was, after all, a senior unit chief within the closest thing America had to a secret police force. And he was not much more than a field agent and her all-too-occasional companion. No one could know what they did together—ever.

She got to her feet and moved towards the bathroom. She knew Trace could see the marks left by his handiwork earlier. She wondered if he felt proud of a job well-done. During the act, she imagined it was important for him to forget who she was. She was his *slut* during their playtimes. As she was walking away, did he allow himself a special satisfaction? Was there recognition of the insanely hard fucking, whipping, and torment he had just given his own boss?

"Jeanette," he called out after her. She stopped and turned to look at him. She was almost back to thinking of him as an employee—another symbol on her organizational chart—but not quite.

"Chief Rogers," he said. "Thank you. And if I can do anything…"

"Trace, you're welcome. And thank you." He got to his feet and approached her. She was slowly gathering her senses and putting back on her stern, flat, business-is-business expression. She was getting back into the *mode.* And it still took some effort to see Trace as not just a hard-cock-rode-well, but as an asset to the organization. She was careful to never allow herself to see him as a lover, really–much less a *friend.* She squinted. Her game face was coming back. She inhaled deeply.

"Go into the office and start a situation room," she commanded. "Gather everything we have on the Hammer case. *Everything.* Those four groups we've been tracking: something has come together in Dallas. I don't think we anticipated this–what's happened. But we're going to need to exercise some of the scenarios we discussed last week. Because... as stupid as it sounded to us up until now, these *fucking* nobodies might just might be getting close. And they're going to need to be discouraged. Heavily...heavily..." Her voice trailed off.

He was in front of her, still nude. She pulled back as he put his arms around her. He gently pulled her to him, his hands tracing a line from her shoulders down to her hips. He cupped her reddened ass and pulled her against his half-hard, still-moist cock.

"Go," she said, roughly pushing him away. She scowled. "GO! Goddamn it! You've got orders!"

In a few moments, he was back in his clothes, his sidearm was in his shoulder holster, and he was out the door and headed to his white Buick with the government plates. As he walked past the surveillance van parked curbside, he hung his still-sweaty ski mask on the side-view mirror and slapped the sliding door twice, letting the guys inside know he was done with the boss. He heard a muffled *whoop!* from inside. He smiled at the corner of his mouth.

Trace was off to Langley just as the shower had gotten warm enough for Jeanette. She admired the marks he had left on her body, the redness. She liked the way it looked in the mirror. But then her mind turned back to work and her teeth started grinding again, like they did almost every day of her life.

PREVIEW

DANGEROUS HARMONY:
Overture

Coming Summer, 2014

http://dangerousharmony.com

John Hammer sat across the table staring deeply into Ashley's eyes and convincing her beyond any doubt that he heard and that he cared.

What's more, he didn't offer suggestions, didn't race to complete her train of thought for her. He just listened compassionately.

Ashley had begun to marvel at this man. If anyone deserved to be a billionaire – and there was still some question in her mind whether anyone did– it was John R. Hammer.

He hadn't always been a billionaire. It was as though at some point he had stood up into a great jetstream of money, and massive amounts of it had magically stuck to him.

And this was how he did it: he *listened.* And the more he listened, the more people opened themselves up to him. He had parlayed that one supreme quality into a network of associates, acquaintances and friends that had helped him to attain the success that they themselves lacked, if only because he seemed so perfect for the role, and he listened.

He appeared to have been let down mainly by his questionable taste in women, combined with a certain fecklessness in regards to dealing with the government.

Ashley completed her story. Buried under a hundred thousand disappointments in the back of her mind, she dug a treasure from the trash. Her chance to survive and thrive was written on the heart of John Hammer.

"Ashley, I want you to know that I feel for what you've suffered. And I..." He winced and shook his head. He had started doing this more frequently with her.

"What was that?" asked Ashley.

"What?"

"That little thing you did with your head."

"It's…" He laughed ruefully, looked off in the distance, and scratched his head. "It's just this: I have started hearing myself talk recently. After years of saying the 'right' thing, I finally started listening to myself. And it's pretty bad sometimes. I guess I sound like I know what's going on, or want people to think I really know what's going on. And the truth is…" He exhaled. "The truth is, Ashley—I just don't know. I don't know about your disorder. I don't know about mine. I'm finally brave enough to admit it. I guess that's what I'm thinking when I do that thing with my head."

Ashley looked at him. Such a curious creature. "So," she asked "what do you feel?"

He looked at her, suddenly puzzled. "I guess I don't know. I don't think I know what I feel."

245

Ashley looked deeply into his eyes. "John, we need to work on that. We need to work on your feelings, because I don't think you've been listening to them. I think you've been listening to everyone else's. And because…I…" Ashley felt a fluttering between her legs. They were coming more frequently now. "…because I think my feelings are telling me something about you. And I wonder if you feel anything like that at all. But before you can answer, you need to know your own feelings, and I don't think that's ever been asked of you."

John just smiled and shook his head. He looked out at the bay from the balcony. He looked out the corner of his eye at Ashley. Ashley felt a flutter. Her confidence with him was increasing. She stood up from the chair and thought what-the-hell and lifted her flowing cover-up, sweetly showing herself to John. He smiled and extended his arm to her. She approached him, a Cheshire grin on her face. Gently, he petted her shaved mound, tracing both sides of her clit. She saw his hips move. He pulled her closer. His chair turned, and next thing she knew, his lips were upon her. His tongue extended to lap at her. This was something new for them. She didn't know he had an interest. She felt her knees quivering. She petted his curly salt-and-pepper hair as he lapped at her sex.

Next thing, he was down on his knee. He took her right leg in his hand and lifted her foot rest on the seat of the chair. This gently opened her more and allowed him to drink from her more closely. She started feeling tantalizing warmth within her. While he gently licked at her, she felt his hand rising up along the inside of her thigh. Two warm fingers started to gently trace lines around her wet entrance while he lapped at her clit.